An Island Far from Home

by John Donahue

Carolrhoda Books, Inc./Minneapolis

Adventures in Time Books

The author wishes to thank Laurence Ward, Suzanne Noonan, and Patrick Donahue for their many helpful comments, and Jill Anderson for her invaluable editorial assistance.

Text copyright © 1995 by John S. Donahue
Cover illustration copyright © 1995 by Mark Anthony

Carolrhoda Books, Inc. c/o The Lerner Group
241 First Avenue North, Minneapolis, MN 55401

LIBRARY OF CONGRESS CATALOGING-IN-PUBLICATION DATA

Donahue, John, 1951–
   An island far from home / by John Donahue.
      p.   cm.
   Summary: The twelve-year-old son of a Union army doctor killed during the fighting in Fredericksburg comes to understand the meaning of war and the fine line between friends and enemies when he begins corresponding with a young Confederate prisoner of war.
   ISBN 0-87614-859-3
   1. United States—History—Civil War, 1861–1865—Juvenile fiction.
[1. United States—History—Civil War, 1861–1865—Fiction.] I. Title.
PZ7.D71473An 1995
[Fic]—dc20   94-9444
                                                                 CIP
                                                                  AC

Manufactured in the United States of America

1 2 3 4 5 6 I/BP 00 99 98 97 96 95

For my wife, Cindy, who helped and encouraged me each step of the way, and for my children, Brendan and Alison

Tilton, Massachusetts
(the present)

It was like any other grandparents' attic, dark and dry and filled with fragments and memories of an era long gone. An old man ducked low beneath the thick, slanting roof beams and led a boy to a dusty trunk hidden in the shadows of the front corner.

"Here it is," the old man said. "Nana wants to bring it to the antique shop before the movers come."

The boy looked down at the massive wooden container. "It's really ancient, Grandpa."

"Yes," the old man replied, "it belonged to my grandfather . . . or great-grandfather."

The boy dropped to one knee and pried his fingers beneath it. "It's heavy," he said, lifting one side sever-

al inches in the air. "We should make sure it's empty."

The old man bent over and lifted the cover. "I can't see anything," he said, staring into an interior as black as a moonless night.

The boy peered into the trunk to check for himself. "What's that?" he asked. He reached in and removed a tiny felt jeweler's box. He pushed open the box with his thumb and smiled. "It's a brass button." He held it up to the light. "And it has the letter *A* on it. What does it stand for?" he asked, handing the button to his grandfather.

The old man searched his memory. "I don't know. I can't think of anyone in the family whose name begins with *A*. But it must have been important to someone."

"Can I have it?" the boy asked.

The old man placed the button back in his grandson's hand. "Of course you can."

The boy looked down at his palm. Even in the dim light, he could see that there was still a luster to the button, as if it had been polished many times. "I wonder why they kept it," he said.

Chapter One

Tilton, Massachusetts (1864)

oshua Loring propped his back against the trunk of the giant maple tree and stretched out his legs. It was late August, and the day was long and hot. He had finished weeding the garden and plucking the heavy, ripe tomatoes from the vines. Now he could relax in the shade. And wait.

From his position he could see the small road that led from the town square to his home. He pulled his father's silver watch from his pocket and checked the time. Half past one. Uncle Robert will be here soon, he thought.

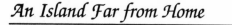

He closed his eyes, and his thoughts began to wander. He was captain of a Union warship that was chasing Confederate raiders off the coast of North Carolina. He was a general, handsome in his dark blue uniform, leading a charge against Robert E. Lee's Army of Northern Virginia. "LORING CAPTURES LEE," the newspaper headlines would blare. Joshua smiled. He would be brave. And famous. And he would get even.

Joshua was roused from his daydream by hoofbeats on the road. Opening his eyes he could see a tall figure on a chestnut stallion galloping toward him. He leaped to his feet and sprinted toward the rider. "Uncle Robert!" he yelled, waving his hands above his head. In the distance the man returned his wave.

When Uncle Robert had dismounted, Joshua led the stallion to a hitching post and, after stroking the huge animal's muzzle, tied him securely.

"So how's my favorite nephew?" asked Robert, pulling a package from his saddlebag.

"I'm your only nephew," Joshua retorted.

"Yeah, but you're still my favorite. You being good?"

"Most of the time," Joshua answered, his blue eyes sparkling. He was tall and strong for a twelve-year-old boy—just like his father, his mother told him often. His hair was reddish brown, and his fair skin was freckled by the summer sun.

Joshua pointed to the bundle under his uncle's arm.

"What's in the package?"

"Think it's something for you?" Robert teased.

"Hope so!"

"Well, we'll just have to go inside and find out."

As Robert walked with his nephew toward the house, a trim figure, dressed in white, appeared at the door. Robert gave Joshua a quick wink. "Enjoying the weather, Catherine?" he called to his sister.

Joshua suppressed a laugh. No matter what the weather was like, his mother did not seem to enjoy it. This had long been a source of amusement for her family. The winters were much too cold, she thought, and the summers much too hot. Spring brought dreary rain and pesky pollen. Only the fall, with its crisp, gentle breezes, seemed to meet with her approval.

"That's enough from you," said Mrs. Loring, trying hard to keep a straight face.

Robert grinned and pulled the package from beneath his arm. "I've brought you a little something," he said.

Joshua let out a sigh. "I thought the package was for me."

"I never said that," Robert chuckled. "But maybe there's something in here for you too."

When they entered the cool darkness of the front parlor, Robert plopped the package down on a table and watched as his sister removed the outer wrapper. Inside were small containers of tea and spices. But that was not all.

"This is for you," said Robert, snatching a finely engraved stationer's box from the package and handing it to Joshua. "But it's yours on one condition: You have to write to me. I realized the other day at mail call that I was the only one who didn't get mail. Here I am, deputy commander of a fort in the middle of Boston Harbor, and I don't get a single letter!"

"You fibber," Mrs. Loring scolded, "I write to you all the time. And we see you twice a month."

Uncle Robert laughed. "Well, anyway, Josh, *you* write to me. I'm only nine miles away, but I get awfully lonely out there on George's Island."

Joshua lifted the lid from the box, and his eyes fell on the most beautiful stationery he had ever seen. Each piece was crisp and white and emblazoned at the top with a picture of Abraham Lincoln surrounded by cannons and flags. Writing letters on paper like this would be a waste, he thought. But a deal was a deal. "I'll write," he promised. "I'll write every week."

Later that afternoon, Joshua and Robert walked slowly down the narrow trail that led to the beach. Robert limped from the leg wound he had received the previous summer at Gettysburg. The sea breezes did little to ease the day's heat, and they wiped beads of perspiration from their faces.

"Uncle Robert, how long will the war go on?" Joshua asked after a time.

"I don't know. I hope it ends quickly. I'd like to

get back to my law practice. And my life."

"The newspapers say it'll be over pretty soon,"
Joshua mumbled dejectedly.

Robert stopped and fixed his deep brown eyes on
his nephew. "What's on your mind, Josh?"

"Well, some regiments have drummer boys. And in
the navy, they have powder monkeys. You can be almost any age, and I was thinkin' maybe I could join
up before it was over."

"Josh," said Uncle Robert, "the war is a terrible
thing. You know that. You've seen the wounded boys
coming home, and you've been to the memorial services. There's very little glory in it. Don't misunder-
stand me. I'm proud to wear my uniform. Just as
your father was. But I wish that I didn't have to."

Joshua stared at his uncle.

"And what about your mother?" Robert continued.
"You need to help her out. There's so much to do,
and I can't be here all the time." Uncle Robert put his
hand on Joshua's shoulder. "Promise me, *promise* me,
Josh, that you won't try to enlist."

Joshua lowered his head and nodded. Tears began
to stream down his cheeks, and he broke away from
his uncle and ran toward the beach. Suddenly he
stopped and spun around. "What about Pa?!" he
yelled. "Who's gonna make them pay for what happened to Pa?!"

Robert approached his nephew. "They're paying

now, Josh," he said softly. "Atlanta and Petersburg are under siege, and we've recaptured Mobile Bay. The South is paying with its blood."

That evening, after Robert had gone, Joshua kissed his mother good night and went to his room. He lit the oil lamp by his bed and carefully placed his new stationery in the top drawer of his desk. He would write his first letter the following day, he decided.

As he lay in bed, he thought about his uncle's visit. He was embarrassed that Robert had seen him cry. Some soldier you are, he thought to himself. One minute you want to join the army, the next you're crying. Maybe he'd better stay home for now. Classes would be starting soon, and he'd have his Lincoln paper to show his friends.

The sounds of night began to filter into his room, and the rustle of the trees whispered a lullaby that rose and fell with each sea breeze. Joshua extinguished his lamp and lay back in the darkness to listen. Soon he was fast asleep.

Chapter Two

Everything in the schoolroom was exactly as Joshua remembered it. The rows of desks were straight and even: five across, five deep. The oak floor gleamed as brightly as the buckle on a general's belt. The stove at the side of the room squatted on short, curved legs, and at the front stood Mr. Rawson's high desk, flanked by two small recitation seats.

Joshua's eyes scanned the back of the room and fell on a seat in the last row by the window. Good, he thought, his favorite seat was still empty. He side-stepped a classmate and bounded toward the spot.

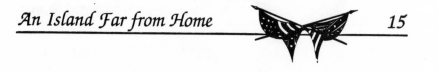

When he reached it, he plunked his belongings atop the desk and, like an explorer of old, claimed it as his own.

The desk was small—too small for a boy of Joshua's size—and he struggled to squeeze his legs under it. But there was no better seat in the classroom. Here, he was as far from Mr. Rawson's booming voice as a student could be, and he was the only one who had a full view out the window. Joshua savored his moment of triumph. He sat back contentedly and gazed out onto the schoolyard.

"Hey, Loring!" a voice snapped beside him. "That's my seat!"

Joshua looked up at the speaker. He was a tall boy, almost as tall as Joshua, and his arms were thick with muscle from working afternoons at the cooper's shop.

"I got here first, Tim. That's Mr. Rawson's rule."

Tim scowled. "I claimed it at the end of last year."

"That doesn't count, and you know it."

Tim leaned over and pushed his face near Joshua's. "If you don't give me the seat, I won't let you into my volunteer regiment."

"What volunteers?"

"I'm calling it Rodgers' Regiment. It'll be a group of boys that'll fight to protect the town if the Rebs ever attack. We'll have drills and uniforms and everything."

The idea intrigued Joshua, but he had no desire to be in any regiment that had Tim Rodgers in command.

And he certainly was not going to give up his seat. "I don't want to be in any boys' regiment," he said. "I'll wait till I'm old enough to enlist, then I'll join the *real* army."

"Yeah?" said Rodgers angrily. "Well, if the Rebs come up here, you're gonna be dead." Then he turned and stalked across the back of the class and threw his cap on a desk at the far corner of the room.

The classroom was nearly full now, and Mr. Rawson was moving about near the door. Joshua pulled his watch from his pocket and checked the time. It was almost nine o'clock, and his best friend, Tom Hogan, had not arrived. He glanced out the window, but there was no one in sight. Hogan's going to be in big trouble, he thought.

Mr. Rawson closed the door to the schoolroom and marched over to his desk. He was a short, plump man with jowls like a hound's. His cheeks were heavily whiskered, and he wore a pair of small, gold spectacles that could easily be overlooked on his large face.

Mr. Rawson looked out over the room and then brought his hickory pointer down on his desk with a crack. The class became silent immediately. "I'd like to welcome back those of you who were here last year," he said, his eyes darting from student to student. "And I bid a warm welcome to those of you who are new to us. I remind you all that we have rules in this classroom that must be obeyed. I insist on it. I shall not tolerate tardiness, unruliness, or speaking out of turn. Is that understood?"

Each member of the class nodded in silent assent.

"You are not primary schoolers," he continued, "you are grammar schoolers, and I expect you to act as such. Agreed?"

Joshua and his classmates again nodded.

"Good!" said Mr. Rawson. "Now that we have that settled, I think this will be an exciting year for all of you. We shall study grammar, composition, reading, spelling, history, map drawing, and declamation. And maybe," he added with a wink, "I shall include a little gymnastics to keep you healthy in body as well as in mind."

Joshua smiled at the thought of Mr. Rawson leading a gymnastics exercise. He wished that Hogan were there to share his amusement.

"Now I ask that you check the top of your desk to make sure that you have a pen and an ink bottle and a slate and a slate pencil. You should also—"

Mr. Rawson was in midsentence when the door to the schoolroom creaked open and a boy with a thatch of black hair peered in.

"Master Hogan!" Mr. Rawson exclaimed. "How kind of you to join us this year. Do you have a note explaining your tardiness?"

The door swung open, and the thin boy stepped into the schoolroom. His dark brown eyes were

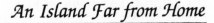

somber and his face deadly serious. "No, sir. Didn't have time to get a note. Had to put out a fire."

Mr. Rawson looked like a triumphant cat who had cornered a mouse. "A fire, you say? And where exactly was this fire?"

"My house."

"I see. And *you* put it out?"

"Helped," said Hogan stoically.

"And that's the truth?"

"Yes, sir. That's the full truth."

Mr. Rawson studied his young student for a moment. "Master Hogan, there are six grammar schools in Tilton. Six. I do not know why Providence has seen fit to put you in my little school. It must be some sort of test. Last year I heard every manner of excuse fall from your tongue. I don't want to hear any more this year. Do I make myself clear?"

"Yes, sir."

"And Master Hogan . . . ?"

"Yes?"

"Next time, your name will be reported to the School Committee."

"Yes, sir."

"Now be seated."

Hogan walked quickly to the back of the classroom and eased into the seat next to Joshua's.

"I can't believe you're late the first day," Joshua whispered.

Hogan smiled and shrugged.

"Was there really a fire at your place?"

"Yup."

"Where?"

"Inside the stove," said Hogan matter-of-factly. "How d'ya think we cooked breakfast this morning?"

Joshua let out a snort of laughter.

"Do you have something amusing to share with us, Master Loring?" Mr. Rawson bellowed from the front of the class.

"No, sir," said Joshua, trying to regain his composure. He glanced at Hogan. His friend's face was as solemn as a preacher's at a funeral. Joshua envied him. With a little bending of the truth, Hogan could get away with just about anything.

Joshua sat back and listened as Mr. Rawson called the class list. Then the morning exercises commenced with a reading from the Bible and a recitation of the Lord's Prayer. The first day of school had officially begun. And Joshua wondered where the year would take him.

Chapter
Three

*A*utumn arrived in Tilton with an explosion of color. The leaves turned a dozen different hues—bright crimsons, rich browns, pale yellows—and the slightest breeze would send a rain of color cascading to the earth.

Joshua strode briskly through this thick, papery carpet on his way to school. On another day he might have walked more slowly, searching the leaves for unusual colors. But this day he had no time for such distractions. He was late, and visions of Mr. Rawson's hickory stick flashed through his mind.

He checked his watch. Five of nine. He still had a

chance to make it. He quickened his pace, jogging along the wooded path that led to the back of the schoolhouse. He checked his watch again. Three minutes of nine. He could do it! His legs began to pump as the schoolhouse came into view. Only a small thicket of trees separated him from the schoolyard. Almost there, he thought. Almost there!

Suddenly there was a loud crashing noise above him, and he was blinded by a shower of small objects falling from the sky. He shook his head and looked down at his clothing. He was completely covered with leaves and dirt. He brushed himself off vigorously and then, still slightly dazed, looked up into the trees.

His gaze was met by peals of laughter, and a voice high above him exclaimed, "'Bout time ya got here, Josh. Been sittin' up here all mornin'."

Joshua recognized the voice immediately. "You'd better stay up there, Hogan. 'Cuz when you get down, I'm gonna whip you!"

There was more laughter amid the branches. "How's a leaf pile gonna whip me?" Hogan yelled.

Joshua looked down at his clothing again. Despite his attempt to brush himself clean, he was still covered with bits and pieces of leaves. He realized how ridiculous he must look. "Just wait and see," he shouted back, trying to salvage some dignity.

"Well, I'm comin' down anyway," Hogan announced. "Pleeease don't hurt me," he added, in mock terror.

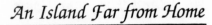

Hogan descended to the lowest branch and dropped to the ground. "How ya doin', Josh?"

Joshua was busy picking at leaf fragments that clung stubbornly to his coat. His hands were filthy. "You're really gonna get it, Hogan," he sputtered.

"We're both gonna get it if we don't skedaddle!" his friend yelled, running toward the schoolhouse. "We're late!"

Joshua had forgotten the time. He shot a glance at his pocketwatch. It was now past nine. "Oh, no," he moaned, and he began to run as fast as his legs would carry him.

Twenty-two students were seated in Mr. Rawson's room, and twenty-two heads turned toward the door as the boys tried to sneak in.

"Not so fast, Master Hogan, Master Loring!" a voice thundered. Joshua felt his heart skip a beat and watched fearfully as Mr. Rawson approached them, slapping his stick against his leg. "I've warned you people about being late and interrupting my class. You'd better have a good excuse for this. And I mean a *good* excuse."

"Yes, sir, we do," Hogan said confidently.

"Yes . . . sir," Joshua stammered, wondering why Hogan sounded so cocky.

"Well, then, why don't you enlighten us?" Mr. Rawson huffed.

Joshua looked at Hogan. "Sir," Hogan began, "I was walkin' down the back path, the shortcut path, when—"

"*Ing,*" Mr. Rawson interrupted. "You were *walking* down the back path."

"Yes, sir. I was walk-*king* down the back path when I seen that Josh had tumbled and hurt his foot. He was all covered with leaves and such, so I stopped to help."

Joshua nodded in agreement. He did not like to lie, but at the same time, he felt a great sense of relief. He would say an extra prayer at Sunday services to make amends.

"I'm real sorry we're late," Hogan continued, "but I thought I was doin' a good deed."

Mr. Rawson squinted at the boys over the top of his spectacles. "The only thing that convinces me that you're telling the truth is that Joshua appears to have taken a fall. Now, Master Loring, if you had allocated sufficient time for your trip to school, perhaps you could have remained on your feet."

"Yes, sir," said Joshua meekly.

"And Master Hogan, I don't care what your excuse is next time. You'll be punished. Now both of you take your seats."

The boys walked to the back of the room and sat down as quietly as possible. Joshua let out a deep breath. They were off the hook.

When all had settled in the room, Mr. Rawson

cleared his throat as he did before making an important announcement. "Ahhem! Ahhhem!" When he
was sure that all eyes were on him, he walked to his
desk and picked up a sheet of paper. "I think I have a
project that might interest you," he said. "This letter
from my son gave me the idea."

Joshua and Hogan exchanged glances.

"I am well aware that many of you have fathers,
brothers, sisters, or other relatives who have answered
our nation's call. As soldiers and as nurses. Many are
living very far away. My own boy is in Virginia with
the Army of the Potomac. I propose," Mr. Rawson
said, pausing dramatically, "that we begin a letter-
writing campaign!"

The class murmured excitedly, but Joshua looked
down at his desk.

"In addition to the letters that you normally send to
your family and friends," Mr. Rawson resumed, "each
week one of you will provide us with the name of
someone in the military with whom you'd like us to
correspond. And we shall flood that fortunate person
with letters."

A feeling of sadness filled Joshua. He did not want
to write to someone else's father. He did not want to
write to anyone except Uncle Robert. And deep within, he feared that the letters would bring back the pain-
ful memories of his own father's death many months
before. As Joshua contemplated Mr. Rawson's project,

he was distracted by a hand waving in the air nearby.

"You have a question, Master Hogan?" Mr. Rawson inquired.

"Yes, sir. How many letters do we got to write each week?"

"Do we *have* to write each week," Mr. Rawson corrected. "Just one."

"And how long does it have to be?"

"However long you wish it."

Hogan turned and whispered to Joshua, "That's not so bad. I can write one letter a week."

Joshua nodded halfheartedly. Maybe it wouldn't be so bad after all, he thought. It might even be funny. He could just picture Uncle Robert at mail call when his name was shouted again and again and again—twenty-four times! "You were the one who wanted letters," Joshua would tell him.

"It's settled then!" said Mr. Rawson. "We will begin our writing campaign this week. The scholars in the front row will make their choices first, and we will work our way to the back."

Joshua looked out the side window. He smiled at the thought of Uncle Robert almost buried in a pile of envelopes. But it would be even better when he became a soldier himself, and the class wrote to him.

Chapter Four

he trouble with girls," said Hogan, "is that they don't know nothin' 'bout politickin'." Joshua agreed.

"My sister Nora was raisin' a ruckus this mornin' 'bout women not havin' the vote. I tried to esplain to her that it ain't natural for girls to vote. But she wouldn't have none of it. She just went on and on 'bout how unfair it all was. And how a woman who reads a newspaper knows just as much as a man. She was ramblin' like a crazy lady."

"You think that's bad," said Joshua, "my ma and her friends were making bandages at the Aid Society last

week, and she said a lot of 'em don't want the war to
go on. Don't even care if we win or lose."

"There," said Hogan, gloating, "that proves it. Girls
just don't know nothin' 'bout politickin'."

It was November 8, election day, and Tilton Square
was bustling. Joshua and Hogan maneuvered through
the crowd, dodging horses and carriages and the heavy
wagons that lumbered toward the railroad station.
They could not wait to find out what was happening in
the election, and in Tilton there was no better place to
learn of the world than at Harrison's Store.

Harrison's sat like a huge wooden block between the
courthouse and the law offices of Fiske and Fiske.
There were other grocery stores in the town, but for
sheer size and assortment of goods, none could match
Harrison's. You could buy just about anything there:
meat, flour, molasses, lard, canned goods, coffee, and
sweets. It even had a small wagon that delivered ice.

"Afternoon, boys!" a voice called the moment they
stepped into the store's cavernous entryway. The
speaker was a beanpole of a man standing behind a
low wooden counter.

"Afternoon, Mr. Harrison," Joshua answered.

"He thinks we're gonna steal somethin'," Hogan
whispered into his friend's ear.

Joshua grinned. He could not remember a single
time that he had entered the store without being
greeted with great enthusiasm by Mr. Harrison. He,

like the other boys in town, had long suspected that the storekeeper's outward display of friendliness was simply his way of saying, *I know you boys are in here, so you better not try to take anything.*

"We just wanted to listen down back," said Joshua, pointing to a group of men near the rear of the store.

"Fine," said Mr. Harrison, a sweet smile pasted on his face, "but remember, if you want to buy anything, I'll be right here."

The boys made their way to the back of the store and found two flour barrels to sit on. Several steps away a half dozen men were engaged in an animated discussion about President Lincoln and his opponent, General George McClellan.

"I don't think McClellan and the Democrats have a chance," said a man who was puffing on a cigar. "Lincoln's got the strength, and this country needs him for a second term."

"Well, there's a lotta people who's sick and tired of war," another responded, "and let's face the facts. Lincoln's gonna fight until the last Reb gives up. No matter how long it takes. I think a lotta people will vote against him."

"And I'm one of them!" said Philip Orcott, the barber, his face burning with emotion. "Think of all our men dying from sickness and wounds on the battlefield. And wasting away in those awful Reb prisons like Libby and Andersonville. We've lost forty men in

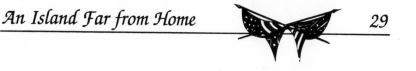

this town so far. Forty men! Things keep up like this, there'll be no one left to run the businesses and do the farming. The Peace Democrats'll end the war and bring the boys home!"

"Mr. Orcott's talkin' like a fool," Hogan whispered.

Joshua dug his fingernails into the sides of the barrel. At that moment he did not care about the prisoners or the wounded or the soldiers in the field. He wanted to tell these men that his father had died and that he did not want the war to end. Not until he had a chance to even the score. He wanted to punish the South, to strike back at it any way he could. He waited, hoping that someone would speak his thoughts for him.

Tom Sandler, the banker's son, pushed himself away from the wall and approached Mr. Orcott. Joshua knew that Tom had been badly wounded at Chancellorsville, in Virginia, and had been discharged from the army on a disability. "I've got a few questions for you, Phil," Tom said. "If we end the war now, what will we have gained? Tens of thousands of men have died fighting the Rebellion, and what will they have died for? Unless we finish the war and crush the Rebels, those men will have died without cause. And the country will never be united."

"I'll tell you what we'll gain," Mr. Orcott said angrily. "We'll save the lives of all the soldiers and sailors still fighting! And we'll save ourselves!"

"And what about the slaves?" Tom persisted. "Unless the South is beaten, slaves'll never be free."

"Who cares about the slaves?" said Mr. Orcott, his voice shaking.

"That's right," said another man. "Those slaves sure ain't worth dying for. It's time we stopped listening to the Abolitionists and started worrying about our own people."

Tom shrugged and returned to his place at the wall. "I thought we were all one people," he said. "Thought that's why we called ourselves a union."

Joshua's spirits soared. You tell 'em, Tom! he thought. You just tell 'em!

The boys sat glued to their barrels, captivated by the words that flew around them. Long after darkness had descended on the square, Joshua pulled his watch from his pocket. "I've got to go!" he exclaimed. "My ma's gonna kill me!" He leaped to his feet and bolted toward the door. But just as he reached for the handle, the door burst open and a small man lunged in. It was Mr. Ames from the telegraph office.

The room grew quiet. Mr. Ames took a deep breath, pulled back his shoulders, and, with all the importance he could muster, announced, "The early returns show that Mr. Lincoln's winning!"

Some of the men in the corner let out a hearty cheer. Mr. Orcott shook his head in disgust. "It ain't final yet," he said.

"I'll be at the telegraph office most of the night," Mr. Ames continued, "so if anyone wants to stop by, I'll keep ya up to date." With that, he turned abruptly and left the store. Joshua and Hogan followed him to the sidewalk.

"Mr. Ames, when will you know the final results?" asked Joshua.

Mr. Ames thought for a moment. "I suspect we'll have a pretty good idea of the winner by early tomorrow. Now, if you boys'll excuse me, I have telegraphs to dispatch."

"I wish we could find out tonight," said Joshua, turning to Hogan.

"Don't worry," said Hogan confidently. "Lincoln's got it easy. I can feel it in my bones."

The following morning Joshua went to the square to see if Hogan's bones were telling the truth. A small crowd had gathered in front of the telegraph office to read a notice tacked to its door. Joshua pressed to the front of the group and scanned the election returns. Although not every ballot had been counted, and in some states the voting was close, it was clear that Lincoln would carry the election. Joshua thrust his fist into the air and shouted in triumph. Old Abe would remain president. And the war would go on.

Chapter
Five

*T*he snowball landed with a *whump!* on Joshua's front steps. Joshua dropped his heavy wooden shovel and wheeled around. Hogan and another boy, Amos Nelson, were running toward him, armed with more snowballs. Joshua jumped off the steps, scooped up a handful of the newly fallen snow, and ran to meet his friends. "Charge!" he yelled, cocking his arm into a throwing position. There was a brief flurry of snow as the boys unloaded their missiles, then all three fell to the ground, laughing.

"Let's play tracker!" Hogan said excitedly.

"Snow's not that deep," said Joshua.

"C'mon, let's play anyway," said Amos.

"Yeah," Hogan urged, "it's deep enough to follow a trail."

"Who's gonna be the Reb?" Joshua asked.

"We'll draw for it," said Amos.

Joshua ran to the side of the road and picked up a long, thin stick. He broke it into three pieces and placed them in his hand so that the length of each was hidden. Hogan chose first and selected a longer stick. "I'm a Union soldier. I'll be General Grant."

Amos was next and, after some hesitation, drew the remaining long stick. "Me, too. I'll be General Sherman."

That meant Joshua was the Confederate soldier. He hated being a Reb, but those were the rules.

"Who are you gonna be?" teased Hogan. "One of them Rebs your uncle's got in prison out on the island?"

Joshua thought for a second. If he had to be a Reb, he would be General Robert E. Lee. "I'll be Lee," he said reluctantly.

"Get outta here, Lee," Hogan growled. "You got exactly three minutes 'fore we come after you!"

Joshua turned and fled through the lightly falling snow into the woods. After several minutes of slipping and sliding on the moist, white ground, he reached his destination—a cluster of boulders that formed a natural fortress. He looked around quickly. They wouldn't attack together, he guessed. They'd come in from different angles. Like good soldiers. And while he was busy with one, the other would try to get him from behind.

He huddled low behind the rocks and frantically packed the snow into small, white balls. Suddenly the silence of the woods was broken by the sound of a snapping branch. Joshua peered above the boulders and surveyed the area in all directions, but he could see no sign of the enemy. His heart began to beat rapidly, and his entire body was filled with excitement. Was this how soldiers felt before battle? he wondered. Maybe this was how his father had felt before the Battle of Fredericksburg, the day he had died. No, this was only a snowball fight. Real soldiers fought for their lives.

Crack! Another branch broke in front of him. Joshua raised his head. In the distance he could see Amos moving cautiously from tree to tree. Hogan was not with him. Joshua turned and peered over the boulders behind him. Still, Hogan was nowhere to be seen. He crouched down as low as he could. He would wait until Amos was closer and then pop up and try to hit him. With Amos out of the battle, it would be an even fight with Hogan.

A snowball whizzed over his head and splattered against the rock behind him.

"Surrender, Johnny Reb!" Amos cried out.

Joshua said nothing. He held his breath and waited for Amos. But where was Hogan?

The sound of Amos's footsteps grew louder. Another snowball exploded against one of the boulders and disintegrated in a white spray. Joshua had waited long enough. He leaped to his feet and fired two snowballs in rapid succession. The first missed Amos by inches. The second thudded into his chest.

"Got you!" yelled Joshua. But his triumph was short-lived. No sooner had he said the words than he felt an icy wallop on the back of his head.

"So much for General Lee!" a voice shouted.

Joshua spun around. There, no more than five feet away, stood Hogan, prepared to hurl another snowball. "If this was a real battle, you'd be dead," Hogan gloated.

"Yeah, well, it was two on one," Joshua mumbled, wiping a clump of snow from his neck. "That's not a fair fight."

Amos and Hogan laughed. "Come on, don't be sore," said Hogan. "It's the same way with the war. The Union army outnumbers the Rebs. Besides, you should be glad we won."

"Well," said Joshua hesitantly, "I guess so."

The snow had almost stopped when the boys trudged back toward Joshua's house.

"I wish someone would answer one o' them letters we been writin'," said Hogan. "Just so we knew they got 'em." Although the class had written to six different soldiers as part of Mr. Rawson's writing campaign, the students had yet to receive a single reply.

"It takes a while for mail to get down to Virginia or Florida," Joshua said.

"Or Mississippi," Amos added.

"I s'pose," Hogan replied. "What names are you gonna give the class?"

"My Uncle Robert," Joshua answered without hesitation.

"My brother Billy," said Amos, who had three brothers in the army.

"How 'bout you?" Joshua asked.

"I'm not sure," said Hogan. "Probably my cousin. He's in South Carolina, I think."

"Well, ya got plenty o' time to decide," said Amos. "By the time Rawson lets us make our picks, the war'll be over."

When Amos and Hogan had gone home, Joshua finished shoveling, then sat down on the top porch step. He could still hear Hogan's words: "If this was a real battle, you'd be dead."

Joshua remembered his father. As he stared in the growing darkness down the front walkway, he thought he could see him, his tall frame dressed in blue, his saber dangling at his side. Time and the new season could not dim the memories that filled Joshua's heart and mind.

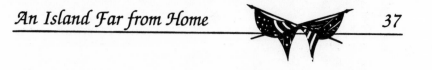

The storm clouds parted, and the first star of the evening appeared in the northern sky. Joshua looked heavenward, breathed deeply in the cold December air, and whispered a prayer for his father.

Chapter Six

othing remained on the kitchen table but empty dishes and the remnants of a Christmas turkey. Uncle Robert pushed his chair back from the table and patted his stomach. "If soldiers got promoted based on their weight, I'd be a general now."

Joshua and his mother laughed.

Robert reached across the table and touched the sleeve of Joshua's brown woolen sweater. "Josh, that's as fine a sweater as I've ever seen."

Joshua glanced at his mother. "Ma gave it to me this morning."

"It's beautiful, Catherine," said Robert. "It must have taken you ages to make."

"Not so long," said Mrs. Loring. "The hardest part was hiding it whenever Josh came home."

"I got some mittens too," said Joshua. "And a penknife with an ivory handle." He reached into his pocket and pulled out a small, shiny knife and passed it to his uncle.

"Now this is a nice piece of work," Robert said. "But what about *my* presents? You don't think I came here just for the fine company and good food, do you?"

Joshua got up from his chair and dashed to the parlor. A heartbeat later he returned with a tiny, wrapped box and dropped it on his uncle's lap. Robert picked up the box and shook it gently. "I think I know what this is," he said, eyeing his nephew. "A saddle! . . . Nope, fishing lures!" he exclaimed as he unwrapped the package. "I should be able to catch a whale with these."

Joshua beamed. "Maybe we can go fishing when the weather gets warmer."

"I'd like that," said Robert. He rose from his chair and hobbled over to the Christmas tree, now ablaze with dozens of candles, and picked up a bundle from beneath it. "Well, I suppose one good turn deserves another," he said, passing the gift to his nephew. "I can't say that I made it myself, but it'll have to do. Happy Christmas, Josh."

Joshua tore the wrapper from the box and studied its thin wood cover. The name "J. Smithers, Optician," was stamped on it. He looked at his uncle quizzically. Did Robert think he needed spectacles? He pried open the slats and sunk his fingers into the mound of straw.

"I don't believe it!" he gasped as he lifted a shiny pair of military binoculars from the container. "They're magnificent!"

"They're just like mine," said Robert. "Good and powerful. And your name's engraved right on them."

Joshua ran to the door and opened it. Frigid air poured into the parlor as he pressed the binoculars to his eyes, adjusted the range, and surveyed the yard. Everything was close and clear, right down to the ripples in the bark of the giant maple tree.

"Close the door this instant!" Mrs. Loring scolded.

Joshua pushed the door shut. "You can see everything as though it's right next to you!" he bubbled. "If the Rebs ever come up here, I'll be able to see them ten miles off!"

"Well, let's hope that doesn't happen," Robert chuckled. "Pennsylvania was close enough."

Joshua thanked his uncle again and then slung the binoculars around his neck.

The day passed much too quickly. When Uncle Robert had an audience, there was no stopping him. One story followed another: the mule that ate the chaplain's hat, the cook who sat on a pumpkin pie, the young private who carried his dog in his knapsack. Joshua had heard them all before, but he could not help but laugh. Only Robert could make him feel this good. This happy.

When day grew into dusk, it was time for Robert to return to Boston. As he pulled his coat from the closet, he said, "Josh, there's something I've been meaning to speak with you about. I've been getting your letters, and I enjoy them very much."

"I've been writing every week," Joshua replied, "just like I promised."

Robert hoisted his coat over his shoulders. "You know we keep Rebel prisoners of war at the fort."

"Sure." Joshua was perplexed by his uncle's statement. Everyone knew there were Rebs at George's Island. Robert had talked about it many times.

"Well, I met someone the other day. A new prisoner who was being processed in. A private named John Meadows. He's from Mobile and was captured after the fall of Fort Morgan in Alabama."

Joshua's eyes were fixed on his uncle.

"The thing is, Josh," Robert continued, "he's about your age, and I got the feeling he's afraid and very lonely." He paused. "I was wondering if, instead of writing to me, you'd be interested in writing to this boy."

Joshua looked at his uncle in disbelief. "He's a Reb!

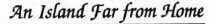

I can't write to a Reb! They killed Pa!" He glanced frantically at his mother. "I'd be a traitor! Right, Ma?"

Mrs. Loring shook her head. "I don't think you'd be a traitor, Josh. But it's up to you."

"That's right," said Robert. "If you don't want to, I won't be angry. You understand that?"

Joshua nodded, still stunned by his uncle's request.

"Why don't you think it over for a while before you decide?" Robert added.

"I don't need to think it over," Joshua said defiantly. "I'm not gonna do it!"

"That's fine, Josh, but if you should change your mind, you can send the letter to me, and I'll make sure he gets it." Uncle Robert finished buttoning his coat and opened the door. He leaned over and kissed his sister, then he turned to his nephew. "Good-bye, Josh. I didn't mean to upset you."

Joshua did not respond. He could not even bring himself to say good-bye. He raced up the stairs to his room and flung himself on his bed. "I won't do it," he said aloud. "I just won't do it!"

Chapter Seven

he morning's horse and carriage traffic had melted much of the snow on the road to Tilton Square. Joshua picked his way around the muddy puddles that dotted the street. It was a beautiful winter's day, brisk and clear, and although the sun held no warmth, it was shining brightly.

Almost two weeks had passed since Uncle Robert's Christmas visit, yet Joshua was unable to shake the name John Meadows from his mind. It was not that he hadn't made a decision about writing the Rebel prisoner. He had made that decision the first night. He would not do it. He could not do it. But he wondered what the boy looked like, how he acted, and how he had felt being in a great battle. John Meadows. The name filled him with a strange mixture of curiosity and loathing. And he thought of it even as he walked toward Hogan's home on this January morning.

Hogan lived in a small, red house only a stone's throw from the railroad station. The area was alive with color, movement, and people. On workdays a steady flow of steam locomotives belched clouds of smoke into the air and pulled crowded passenger cars between Rhode Island and Boston. On Sundays families dressed in their finest gathered at the station for excursions to Boston and beyond.

Joshua passed the station house but did not look in. Instead, he made his way across the tracks and up the narrow walkway that led to Hogan's home. His friend was waiting on the porch, a newspaper clutched in his hand. "Hurry up and see what I got!" he yelled.

Joshua climbed the steep porch steps, stamped his boots dutifully, then followed his friend through the house to his bedroom.

"Look at this," said Hogan, flashing the newspaper in front of him. "It's got pictures of the Battle o' Nashville!" Hogan had the largest newspaper collection Joshua had ever seen, and he had worked hard for every one of them. Each morning he rose at the break of day to unload stacks of papers from the morning

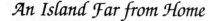

mail train. He was paid three cents for his work and was given a free newspaper. He had saved hundreds of them.

Joshua and Hogan pored over the illustrated paper, studying each picture and commenting on the strategies of battle and the bravery of the Union troops at Nashville.

"Boy, General Hood really got licked," said Joshua, studying the battle maps.

"Yeah," said Hogan contentedly, "and General Thomas and his cavalry are gonna chase 'em down. They got 'em on the run now."

The boys looked at the newspaper for a few more minutes, and then Joshua sat back. "You have any papers 'bout the battle at Fort Morgan?" he asked.

"In Alabama?"

"Yeah."

"Sure," said Hogan. "What do you wanna look at them for? That's old news."

"No special reason," said Joshua, shrugging. "I was just curious."

Hogan dragged a stack of papers from beneath his bed. "Here it is!" he announced after a brief search. "It was last summer." He passed the paper to Joshua, who began to skim through it.

"What's it say?" Hogan asked.

"You know," said Joshua haltingly, "it just tells about the battle."

"I know that. But what does it *say?*"

Joshua read more slowly. "Well, it says that Fort Morgan was one of the forts that guarded the entrance to Mobile Bay. And when Admiral Farragut tried to sail the Federal ships into the bay, the Rebs opened fire on 'em. After the Union sailors beat the Reb navy, soldiers landed and laid siege to the fort."

Joshua began to read the article word for word. "'The garrison at the fort, which consisted of artillery-men from Alabama and Tennessee, stood their ground as the Federal troops moved into position. Finally, on August 22, the Federal guns let loose a mighty roar, and over three thousand cannonballs were hurled at the fortress. The following day the white flag was raised, and the Rebels surrendered the fort. Over five hundred prisoners were taken.'" Joshua closed the paper and returned it to Hogan. "That musta been some battle," he said. "We shot three thousand cannonballs at those Rebs."

"Yeah," said Hogan, carefully returning the paper to the stack. "I bet we killed a bunch of 'em."

"It must have been scary, being surrounded and all."

Hogan did not answer. Instead he pushed his nose in the air and began to sniff like a hound who had caught the scent of a rabbit. The sweet smell of freshly baked bread had begun to waft through the house. "Come on," he said, "let's get somethin' to eat."

Joshua and Hogan followed the aroma to the kitch-

en, where they found Hogan's older sister, Nora, standing near the stove.

"Joshua Loring!" Nora exclaimed. "I didn't know you were here. Tommy, why didn't you tell me my favorite fellow was visiting?"

Joshua felt the blood rise in his cheeks. He liked Nora. With her long, brown curls and eyes the color of the winter sea, she was one of the prettiest girls in Tilton.

"Yeah, well, if Josh is your favorite fella, what about Pat?" said Hogan, smiling.

Patrick O'Rourke was Nora's fiancé. He was fighting with the famous Irish Brigade of the Union Army.

Nora put her arm around Joshua and gave him a squeeze. "Well, Pat's far away," she said, "but Josh is right here."

"I don't believe it!" said Hogan, exploding in laughter. "She's makin' you turn all red, Josh."

"Well, maybe I'll join the army soon," said Joshua, trying to regain his composure.

Nora smiled and released her grip. "Then I'll have two men in the army, and I'll be the luckiest girl in Tilton."

Hogan rolled his eyes toward Joshua. "She's crazy," he said half seriously.

The boys took their seats at the kitchen table and were treated to slices of hot bread and marmalade.

"Did you write your letter for school yet?" asked

Hogan as he wolfed down his snack.

"Nah," Joshua answered, "I have to do it tonight."

The boys were now in the eleventh week of Mr. Rawson's writing campaign, and responses from the soldiers were beginning to arrive.

"Mary's brother sent a good letter," said Hogan.

"Yeah," Joshua agreed, "it was real good." He put his head back and stared at the ceiling. "What would happen if someone in town wrote to somebody really strange?"

"What do you mean 'strange'?" Hogan asked.

"You know, like if they wrote to a Reb or someone like that."

"Wrote to a Reb?!" Hogan almost choked on his bread.

"Yeah."

"How would the letter get delivered?"

"Just suppose it could."

Hogan thought for a second and then said, "They'd be hung. No doubt about it. Anyone who'd do that would be a traitor, and they'd be hung."

"I guess that would be the best thing to do," Joshua agreed.

"That would be the *only* thing to do," Hogan corrected. Hogan looked at Joshua, then his face broke into a broad grin. "Who'd ever be crazy 'nuff to write to a Reb anyway?"

Joshua shrugged. "No one," he said.

Chapter Eight

oshua stoked the log in the fireplace and watched the embers flicker like lightning bugs as they drifted down onto the hearth. He pulled a long piece of wood from the basket near his feet and placed it gently on the irons. "I'll have to bring in some wood later," he said, more to himself than to anyone else.

Mrs. Loring put down her sewing and looked up. "I think we'll need it."

Joshua returned to his chair and began to read.

"How's your book?" his mother asked.

"Good."

"Still reading *The Deerslayer?*"

"Ma, I finished that a week ago," he said, a hint of irritation in his voice. "I'm reading *The Last of the Mohicans* now."

"I didn't know that," said Mrs. Loring. "I don't keep a record of when you finish one book and start another."

Joshua ignored his mother's remark. He looked down at his book but found himself unable to concentrate. The words seemed to dance on the pages, moving up and down as if they were playing tag with his eyes. He slammed the cover shut and dropped the book to the floor. "I'm not gonna write that Reb," he pronounced suddenly, as if he and his mother had been discussing the matter all evening. "Never!"

"That's fine, Josh," said Mrs. Loring, startled by his outburst. "Robert won't be angry."

Joshua knew his uncle would not be mad, but for some reason he felt compelled to explain his decision. "I'd be a traitor if I wrote to him. Like Benedict Arnold. And they'd hang me!"

Mrs. Loring looked closely at her son. "I don't think you'd be a traitor."

"Well everyone else sure would," he answered, his voice rising.

"Not everyone, Josh. Not everyone."

The confusion and anger that had built within Joshua over the previous two weeks erupted in a

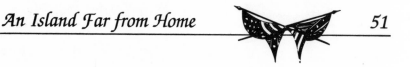
tirade. "They killed Pa!" he said furiously. "How can you stick up for them?! How can you be a Reb-lover?! If Pa was alive he'd never do it!"

A flash of pain crossed Mrs. Loring's face. She reached across the short distance that separated her from her son and took his arm. "That's not fair, Josh. You can't begin to understand my feelings for the Rebels. They've changed my life more than you'll ever know."

Joshua looked down at his mother's hand. Already he was ashamed by his outburst.

"As for your father," Mrs. Loring continued, "I can't say what he would want you to do. I do know that he treated every man as a human being, whether that man was a friend or an enemy." Mrs. Loring rose from her chair and walked to the hutch. She reached to the top shelf and pulled down the tin box that Joshua knew contained his father's letters. Many evenings when he had come down from his bedroom to kiss his mother good night, he had found her with the box open on her lap, letters spread about her. Now he watched her search carefully through the tin and return with a thick envelope.

"There's something I want to read to you," she said, opening a letter with heavily creased pages. "Your father sent it from Virginia." Mrs. Loring leaned back in her chair and began:

My Dearest Catherine,

*I am writing to you by candlelight outside
my tent, so if I misspell then that is the reason.*

*It is quiet here now and quite beautiful. I
am safe and well, but I miss you and Joshua
so. I know that although we are many miles
apart we share the same sky and the same
stars. So when you read this letter, look to
the sky, and maybe, in one of the stars, you
will see my reflection.*

Mrs. Loring paused and took a deep breath.

*Yesterday we fought the Rebels in a small
woods nearby, and when the fighting had
ended I went in with my aides to minister to
the wounded. It was a fearful sight. We carried the injured, both our boys and the Rebels, to the ambulance wagons and brought
them to the field hospital. I operated almost
all night.*

*I pray that this war ends soon and that
Joshua may live his life without seeing the
horrors that I have seen.*

Mrs. Loring's eyes filled with tears, and she read the
rest of the letter to herself. When she finished, Joshua
took her hand in his. "Don't cry, Ma," he said.

She brushed the tears from her cheeks. "Your father
was a good and decent man. And he helped anyone

who needed his help. Even if that person was a Rebel. And when you talk of that young prisoner at George's Island, I don't think of a Rebel soldier. I think of a boy like you."

Joshua lowered his head and held his mother's hand as tightly as he could.

Chapter Nine

*T*hat night Joshua could not sleep. He propped himself against the headboard of his bed and pulled his blanket and quilt tightly around him. Although he was alone, the room was filled with movement. The January moon filtered through the barren tree branches outside his bedroom window, creating silhouettes on the wall in front of him. And with each breeze, the silhouettes performed an eerie dance.

Joshua stared at the swaying patterns as they moved back and forth, to and fro. His mind replayed the day's events again and again. Things just didn't make sense anymore. Like Hogan, he had always thought that having anything to do with a Reb was just plain wrong. And helping one, well, that was downright traitorous. Everyone knew that.

But he could not forget his father's letter. Pa had helped wounded Rebels. Had helped them on the battlefield, even though they had been trying to kill him. That was a hundred times worse than writing a letter to one. And no one, not Hogan, not anyone, could call his father a traitor.

And what about Uncle Robert? Why didn't Robert hate John Meadows? And all the Confederates? They had almost killed him at Gettysburg. His leg would never be the same. Why would Robert want him to write to a Rebel soldier?

Joshua drew his knees to his chin and wrapped his arms around his legs. He didn't know what to think anymore. Things had been so much clearer before. Now everything was so . . . so muddled. He thought long and hard. Then he made his decision. He would write one letter. Just one. He would do it for Uncle Robert. And none of his friends would ever know.

He swung his feet over the side of the bed and lit the lamp on his nightstand. It was bitterly cold, and in the glow of the lamp, he could see his breath. He stood up, pulled his quilt over his shoulders, and walked to his desk.

The stationery that Uncle Robert had given him last

summer was still in the top drawer. With its flags and cannons and picture of Old Abe Lincoln, it would be perfect for the letter he was going to write. He removed a fresh sheet from the stack and placed it before him. Then he closed his eyes and thought. He would make it a short letter. Very short. He dipped his pen in the ink bottle and began.

Dear John Meadows,

Joshua realized his mistake the moment he lifted his pen from the paper. He could not possibly call John Meadows "Dear." He crumpled up the paper, annoyed that he had wasted it, and drew another sheet from his desk. He began again.

Private John Meadows:

That sounded better, he thought. Much better.

My name is Joshua Loring and I live in Tilton, Massachusetts. My uncle, Major Robert Pennington, said I should write you.

Joshua paused. He would make sure that John Meadows knew he was no Reb-lover.

My pa got killed at Fredericksburg so I don't much like Rebs. But seeing that you're not fighting any more I think it's probly all right to write you.

Then he paused again. He did not want to tell John Meadows that he was in school. After all, the young Southerner was a soldier who had fought in a great battle.

> *I'm joining the army as soon as I can. I already own a pair of army binoculars. I just hope the war doesn't end before I get my chance.*

Joshua stopped and reread what he had written. That sounded good, he thought. There was no way that anyone would think he was a traitor. He signed the letter simply,

Joshua Loring

He folded the note and placed it in an envelope that he addressed to his uncle. Then he extinguished his lamp and climbed back into bed. He felt better now. His letter would satisfy his uncle and his mother, and he would not have to write again.

The following morning, before posting his letter, Joshua added one sentence. He asked, "What was it like at Fort Morgan?"

Chapter Ten

"C'mon, Josh!" Hogan yelled. "Move it!"

Hogan walked surefootedly over the ice of Latten's Pond. Joshua trailed behind him, lugging a sled with two stools and a fish bucket atop it. He planted each foot firmly in front of him but still had trouble maneuvering over the pond's slippery surface.

"C'mon!" Hogan yelled again. "You're walkin' like a ninety-year-old lady."

Joshua took his eyes off the ice to glare at his friend. "Easy for you to say, Hogan. If you fall you only have two inches to go down. I'm twice as tall as you are."

"Sound just like an old lady, too!" snickered Hogan as he glided further ahead.

Joshua quickened his pace. He was not about to let Hogan make fun of him and get away with it. He skimmed over the frozen water until the distance between them was cut to several feet. But just as he was about to give Hogan a playful shove, his legs began to slide back and forth, and his feet flew up in front of him. A fraction of a second later, he felt the crunch of the frozen snow beneath him as his backside landed squarely on the ice. "Ohhh," he moaned.

Hogan wheeled around, startled by the crashing noise behind him. "You all right?" he asked. "Josh, you all right?"

"I feel like I broke in two," Joshua muttered as he lay on the ice. Hogan extended his hand. Joshua took it and sat up slowly. "Ohhh," he moaned again. "I feel like I got paddled a thousand times."

When he saw that Joshua was not hurt, Hogan began to giggle. "Must o' been a nice dance ya did there. You should be in one o' them acrobatic shows." Hogan could not pass up the opportunity to tease his friend. He looked down at the ice and clumped one foot carefully in front of the other, as if walking a tightrope. Then he stopped short, thrashed his arms wildly in the air, spun around, and plopped down on the ice. "Ohhhhhhh," he moaned, mimicking Joshua's cry.

Despite his discomfort, Joshua laughed. "You're

gonna get it, Hogan!"

Hogan and Joshua pulled themselves to their feet. "From now on, I'll pull the sled," Hogan announced. "You got a hard 'nuff time just walkin'."

The boys chose a spot near the center of the pond. Hogan dragged the stools from the sled. "You wanna sit?"

"Nah, I'll stand for a while," Joshua answered with as much dignity as he could muster.

Hogan began to chip at the ice with a small hand ax. "Someday, I'm gonna get me somethin' heavier to do this," he grunted as he hacked deeper into the frozen surface. Joshua watched him work for several moments and then looked about.

Latten's Pond was on a farm near the outskirts of the town. It was over a hundred yards across and was surrounded by towering pine trees that were now capped with snow. Joshua had gone there for as long as he could remember. Mr. Latten had just two rules: no cutting timber and no setting fires.

"Hey, you cured enough to give me a breather?" panted Hogan. "This ice is thick." Hogan had dug three or four inches into the ice but had not yet reached water.

Joshua took the ax from him and began to hit at the small pit that Hogan had made. After working steadily for several minutes, Joshua felt the ice give way beneath the sharp tip of the ax. He had broken through. The boys enlarged the hole and smoothed its rough edges.

"There's some big bass down there," said Hogan, drawing his stool closer to the hole. "Tim Rodgers was here last week with his brother, and they caught some huge ones."

"That's humbug," said Joshua as he baited his fishing line. "If Tim told you he caught a whale, you'd believe him."

Hogan tied a sinker to his line and dropped it into the blackened hole. "Yeah, well, we'll find out." The boys twisted their lines around their arms, sat back on their stools, and stared down into the hole. "You ever seen a whale?" asked Hogan.

"Just pictures."

"My pa knows a man from Nantucket," Hogan continued, "who spent four years chasin' whales in the South Seas."

Joshua whistled.

"They had whales bigger than boats down there. With so much oil in 'em you could light a million lamps. And if one attacked you, that was the end. You'd be dead. Don't matter how big your harpoon was, the whale would get you. And you know what else? They got savages down there that don't wear no clothes."

"No clothes at all?"

"Nope."

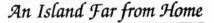
"Well, they sure would if they lived here." Joshua laughed and pulled his coat tighter around him.

"Maybe someday I'll go on a whalin' trip," said Hogan dreamily. "That would be somethin'."

The boys continued to watch their lines for movement, but the lines were as straight and still as soldiers at attention. After a time, Joshua went to the sled and brought back a piece of cheese and some bread that his mother had packed. He shared it with Hogan.

"You gonna go to the high school?" Joshua asked, settling back on his stool.

"Don't know. My folks don't come from money like yours, Josh. I might have to go work for the railroad or the shoe factory. Besides, my pa says there's no point in an Irish boy gettin' all schooled. Couldn't get a fancy job anyway."

Joshua knew there was truth in what Hogan said. There were businesses in Tilton where the Irish could not even apply for jobs. It was strange, he thought, that Irish immigrants were considered good enough to fight and die for their new country, but were not good enough to work in many places. "Is that what you want to do?" he asked. "Work in some factory?"

Hogan shrugged. "Who knows? How 'bout you?"

"I might take the high-school entrance examination next year. If I don't join the army first."

Hogan's eyes grew wide. "You're big enough to enlist, Josh," he said excitedly.

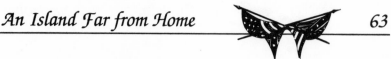

"How 'bout if we join up together," said Joshua. "You're a real good fighter."

Hogan shook his head. "Nah, they'd never let me in, 'cause I'm so small, but you could fool 'em and say you were older."

"Maybe," said Joshua cautiously, "but sometimes the recruiter makes you swear you're eighteen. How am I gonna do that?"

"Easy! Some fellas just write in the number 18 on a piece of paper and stick it in the bottom of their shoe. Then when the recruiter asks 'em how old they are, they just say they're over 18. It ain't even lyin'!"

Joshua smiled.

"I seen the recruitin' posters at the station," Hogan went on. "They pay sixteen dollars a month now! And a bounty for enlistin', too! And you could kill some Rebs before the war ends!"

"Yeah, maybe I'll do just that!"

Hogan nodded vigorously.

Joshua pulled his line from the water to see if the bait was still there and then let it fall back into the hole. "There's nothing down there," he said glumly. "I was hoping I'd catch something for when my Uncle Robert comes tonight."

Hogan bobbed his line. "Your uncle still at that fort on George's Island?"

"Yeah."

"Maybe we could visit sometime and take a look at

the Rebs they got there."

"I think you gotta be a soldier to get on the island," said Joshua uneasily.

"That's too bad. I'd sure like to tell them Rebs what I think o' them."

As the morning wore on, the winter winds bit into the boys' exposed skin, and they hunched forward to protect themselves from the cold. They still had not gotten so much as a nibble on their lines.

"I told ya Tim Rodgers is a liar," said Joshua through chattering teeth. No sooner had the words parted his lips than he felt a powerful tug on his line—a tug that nearly jerked him from his stool. He leaped to his feet and held the line so tightly it almost cut through the outer layer of his mittens. Hogan dropped his own line and stepped to Joshua's side. The fight was on.

"C'mon," Hogan shouted, "let's run back, and we'll pull 'im out." Hogan grabbed the line closer to the hole, and the boys scrambled backward, straining against their unseen enemy. Two, three, four feet of line were dragged from the water.

"We nearly got 'im!" Joshua yelled. "Just a little more!" But as quickly as the tugging had started, it stopped, and the boys almost tumbled over backward as the line went slack.

"Fiddle!" Hogan exclaimed.

Joshua frowned. He walked over to the hole and pulled out what was left of his line. The hook, sinker, and bait were gone. "I don't believe it," he muttered. "He got my good hook." He peered back into the hole. "Wonder what that was?"

"Something really big," Hogan said, chuckling. "Maybe a whale." Joshua grabbed Hogan and wrestled him to the ice.

"So is Tim Rodgers a liar now?" Hogan teased.

"Yeah," said Joshua, smiling, "he's still a liar."

The boys climbed to their feet, packed their gear on the sled, and began the long, cold walk home. As soon as they reached the shore, Joshua lengthened his stride. He wanted to escape the biting wind. And he wanted to make sure he was at home when Uncle Robert arrived.

Chapter
Eleven

The snow was falling lightly when Uncle
Robert climbed the porch steps, favoring
his bad leg. His hat and coat were salted
heavily with fine, white crystals, and his
cheeks were reddened by the frigid air. It was his first
visit to Tilton since Christmas.

Joshua felt uneasy. He knew that Robert must have
received his letter, and he wondered if he had passed it
on to John Meadows. And if the young Confederate
had responded. It was queer, he thought. He was
afraid that the Rebel had answered his letter, but at the
same time he was afraid that he had not. Now Robert

was here, and his question would be answered.

"We didn't know if you'd come this evening, it's so cold out," said Mrs. Loring as she helped her brother out of his coat.

"And miss a home-cooked dinner?" joked Robert. Then he added seriously, "It's been just awful on the island. The winds never seem to die down. You know, as odd as it sounds, I'd almost rather be down south again."

As soon as Robert had settled in front of the fire-place, Mrs. Loring started to pepper him with questions. What was happening in Boston? she asked. Had he been to any plays? Or music recitals? Or parties? One question was followed by another and yet another. Joshua smiled. He was glad to see his mother so happy and to hear her voice so lively. He remembered when it had always been so, but those times seemed ages ago.

The longer Robert talked, the more anxious Joshua grew. He had hoped his uncle would make some mention of the letter. But, although he talked of almost everything else, the name John Meadows was never spoken.

For a time Joshua debated whether to ask him outright if he had heard from the young prisoner. But he decided against it. He did not want to seem too eager, and besides, he thought, why should he care if some Reb decided to write to him? He would just put the whole matter out of his mind.

When dinner was finished, Uncle Robert rose from the kitchen table and disappeared into the parlor. A moment later he returned, carrying an envelope. "I almost forgot, Josh, this is for you."

Joshua's heart started to pound. "Did you read it?" he asked.

"No, I didn't."

Joshua examined the envelope. His name was written on the front in small, neat script. He opened it and began to read to himself.

Joshua Loring,

I don't much cotton to Yankees, but seeing that I'm in prison and all, I guess it's not too bad for me to write. I'm 14 years old and I got a mother, father, two sisters and a dog named Tan. I used to live in Mobile and went to the Center School. Someday, I'm going back. Fort Morgan was real hard fighting but we did pretty good. It took a lot of Yankees to make us surrendur. I didn't want to. Some of my friends got killed there. It hurt real bad to see that. I'm sorry about your pa. Terrible things happen sometimes.

Do you like fishing and do you like snowball fights? Do you got any pets?

Private John Meadows

When Joshua finished he looked up at his uncle. "You want to read it?"

"No, I told Private Meadows I wouldn't. Like I said, it's for you."

"How did he feel about . . . you know, about writin' to me?"

"Well, let's just say at first he was about as excited as you were. But I told him it was just a letter and nothing more. He thought about it for a few days and then said all right."

"Am I supposed to write back?" Joshua asked.

"It's up to you."

"I don't know if I will. I'll have to think on it."

"That's fine," said Robert. "And if you decide to, you can write him directly."

Before going to bed, Joshua huddled near the fireplace and reread John Meadows' letter until he knew its words by heart. He tried to picture what the young Rebel looked like and how it must have been for him at the Battle of Fort Morgan, where he had fought for his life and watched his friends die. "That Reb must be sort of brave," he said to his mother.

"I should imagine so," said Mrs. Loring, as she paged through her newspaper.

"Maybe I'll write just one more letter." Joshua stared at the flames leaping in the fireplace. "Ma, you know anyone who's ever been to Alabama?"

"No," Mrs. Loring replied, "I can't say that I do."

"I was wondering what it's like down there."

"Well, it's supposed to be warm, and I . . . I just don't know that much about it, Josh."

"They got slaves there, don't they?"

"Yes, some people do. It's cotton country."

"I heard some men in town saying that slavery isn't that bad, because the slaves are cared for by their masters and they can't take care of themselves."

Mrs. Loring put down her newspaper. "Those men are wrong," she said. "How would they feel if another man owned them? How would they like it if someone could decide every detail of their lives and could sell them like horses or cows?"

Joshua shook his head. "They wouldn't."

"If you own someone," Mrs. Loring said, "you take away his dignity and his dreams. That's a horrible thing."

"Do you think the Negroes are equal with us?" Joshua asked.

Mrs. Loring hesitated. "Well . . . whether they're equal or not, they're entitled to live as free men and women."

"I wonder if John Meadows owns slaves," said Joshua.

"I don't know," said Mrs. Loring, "but I think the president has made sure that the era of slavery is over."

Joshua nodded. He had read Lincoln's Emancipation Proclamation in school, and he knew that the slaves had been freed in those areas of the South still in rebellion. But he knew, too, that their freedom would not become a fact until the Union Army arrived. "Pa died to free the slaves, didn't he?"

"That was surely one reason," said Mrs. Loring. "But I think he died for many reasons. He opposed slavery very much. And he wanted to keep the country together. To preserve the Union. At the same time, he wanted to be with all the other men who joined the army. His friends. He wanted to be their regimental surgeon in case they were wounded or sick. And that is what put him on the battlefield."

Joshua thought for a moment. "Maybe John Meadows just wanted to be with his friends, too."

"I suppose that's possible," said Mrs. Loring. "Sometimes our enemies are very much like ourselves."

Chapter Twelve

he sound of children's voices drifted over the schoolyard, a high-pitched babble that mingled with the rustling of tree branches. Joshua stood amidst a shivering group of classmates and tightened his scarf. Although he usually savored his last moments of freedom before school, this day he could not wait to escape the bitter air that stung his cheeks.

At precisely 8:45 A.M., Mr. Rawson appeared at the door, carrying a bell in one hand and his hickory stick in the other. He lifted his arm high in the air and began to ring the bell in a steady rhythm. "Come now, scholars! Let's move with vigor!" he called, his jowls jiggling with each movement of his arm.

At his command, the students lined up at the door.

"Too bad Rawson didn't get drafted," Hogan whispered as they marched into the schoolhouse. "Just have him start yappin' on the battlefield, and them Rebs would surrender lickety-split."

Joshua smiled. He would never have admitted it to Hogan, but he actually liked Mr. Rawson. Although his teacher was strict, he was fair and didn't play favorites. And he had always gone out of his way to help Joshua whenever he needed it.

After the class had settled in and recited their morning prayer, Mr. Rawson strode to the front of the room. "Before we begin our grammar, there are several matters I wish to bring up. First, I have something to show you." He retrieved a paper from his desk and with great flourish waved it in front of the class. "We have received yet another reply from our writing campaign. Anne Howard's brother," he said, gesturing toward a young girl with neatly braided hair, "has sent us correspondence from Virginia. His letter describes camp life and the campaign at Petersburg."

Mr. Rawson leaned back against his desk and began to read. It was as if Anne's brother were right there in the classroom speaking to them. He told of drills and marches, and evenings by the campfire, and of hardtack so tough it would almost break your teeth. And he told of how one night he and a friend had sewn up the legs of a new recruit's trousers, so that when reveille sounded the following morning, the recruit had to hop through camp to the inspection line. But not all of the letter was so funny. Anne's brother also wrote of his company's attack on a Confederate supply train and how one of his friends had been wounded. The class grew quiet, and even Hogan's face became serious.

When Mr. Rawson finished reading the letter, he folded it and returned it to Anne. "Now," he said, breaking the silence, "I believe that it is Master Lyttle's turn to select a candidate for our writing project."

Caleb Lyttle, a short, pale boy sitting two rows in front of Joshua and Hogan, stood up and walked to the front of the room. He shifted his weight nervously from one foot to the other. "I'd like everyone to write to my pa," he said. "He's a lieutenant in the Massachusetts Colored Infantry."

A few children in the class began to giggle. "He ain't colored!" Tim Rodgers blurted. "He's as white—"

"Shhh!" Mr. Rawson glared at Tim over the top of his spectacles. Turning to the younger student, he said, "Very good, Master Lyttle. Very good, indeed. Can you tell the class something about the colored infantry?"

"Yes," the boy answered. Despite the earlier laughter he was growing more comfortable in front of the

class. "Some regiments are made up of all Negro soldiers. 'Cept for the officers. They're mostly white. My pa's an officer."

"I heard about them coloreds," Hogan whispered to Joshua.

Joshua had too. He had read about the regiment of colored infantry Colonel Robert Gould Shaw had formed in Boston. Colonel Shaw and many of these Negro soldiers had been killed in a failed attack on Fort Wagner, in South Carolina.

A dark-haired girl raised her hand. "Are the colored soldiers slaves?" she asked.

"No," said Caleb, "some used to be slaves, but they escaped. And some were free men before the war."

Mr. Rawson was obviously pleased with Caleb's choice. "Maybe we can learn more of the colored soldier by writing to your father," he said. Caleb smiled and gave his father's address to the class.

After school, Joshua and Hogan strapped their books and began their walk home.

"I started writing to someone on my own," said Joshua as they drifted toward the square.

"Who?"

"A soldier."

"Where's he garrisoned?"

"Boston."

"Oh," said Hogan. It was common knowledge among the boys in the class that there was a pecking order when it came to corresponding with soldiers. Writing to a soldier in Boston simply did not carry the same status as writing to a soldier in Virginia or Georgia—or anywhere in the South, for that matter.

"How come you're writin' to him?" Hogan asked.

"My Uncle Robert asked me to. He knows him."

"Was he in any battles?"

"Don't know," Joshua lied.

"You should ask him. He could have some good stories!"

"Maybe I will," said Joshua, "next time I write."

In the distance the boys could see the thin steeple of the church rising above the square. They passed the blacksmith's shop and the express company and the other small businesses that lay on the outskirts of the town. As they approached the square, a foreign sound split the air. *Ratta-ta-tum-tum-tum. Ratta-ta-tum-tum-tum.* The boys stopped, transfixed by the staccato beat. A single drum tapping in the afternoon meant only one thing: A recruiter had arrived.

Chapter Thirteen

oshua and Hogan reached the town square just as the drumbeat ended. A dozen men had gathered around a short, fierce-looking officer who was standing on the courthouse steps. A young soldier, his drum slung low in front of him, stood at attention behind his commander.

"Men of Tilton!" the officer shouted. "I am Captain Lige of Colonel Wharton's Light Cavalry. This is your opportunity to join the finest unit in the field: Wharton's Light Cavalry! We are recruiting able-bodied men between the ages of eighteen and thirty-five and will supply them with horses, arms, and equipment."

"What kind of bounty would we get for enlisting?" a tall man in the crowd yelled out.

"If you enlist for a term of three years, you'll receive a state bounty of $125 and a town bounty of $100. Just think of what you can do with that kind of money!"

"Can't do nothin' with it if you're dead," another man shouted back. "'Cept buy yourself a nice send-off!"

The men in the crowd laughed, and even the officer's lips creased in a smile. "That's quite true," the captain continued, "but I'll tell you this: You'll make out a lot better if you enlist today than if you wait for your name to come up in the draft. I have a table set up in the lobby of the courthouse. Anyone interested in joining the finest outfit in the army should stop by and see me." The captain gave the men a quick look, did a sharp about-face, and disappeared into the courthouse. The young soldier followed him, tapping on his drum. *Ratta-ta-tum-tum-tum. Ratta-ta-tum-tum-tum.*

"We've sent enough of our boys to the war," an older man said when he was sure the officer could not hear him. "Let 'im go to some other town."

"I'll take my chances with the draft," said a man whom Joshua recognized from the bakery. "I got a business to run. I can't up and leave it for three years."

"Those bounties for joinin' up ain't so good anyways," said one of the men who had shouted at the

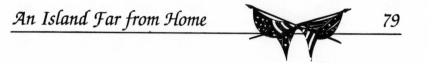
officer. "Besides, some men are willing to pay a lot of money for you to fight in their place. I hear substitutes in New York can get a thousand dollars."

"A thousand dollars," a dairyman whistled. "You could almost buy a small farm with that." A number of the men nodded in agreement, and after a few minutes of discussion, they began to disperse. Not a single one followed the captain up the courthouse steps.

Joshua watched silently. He could remember when the recruiting lines were long and there was an unending supply of young men. How things had changed.

"This is your chance, Josh," Hogan said, giving his friend a stiff elbow to the ribs.

"What?"

"Your chance! This is your chance!"

A wave of panic surged through Joshua. "You . . . you got to be eighteen, Hogan," he sputtered. "You heard him."

Hogan glanced around. "Ain't nobody else interested. I bet they'd bend the rules for you. And you could use that trick I told you about puttin' the number in your shoe." Hogan began to push Joshua toward the steps.

"C'mon, Hogan. Cut it out!"

Hogan stopped short and thrust his face up to Joshua's. "Hey, you're the one always jawin' about joinin' up and fightin'. So how come when your chance comes, you turn yella?"

Joshua glared at his friend. But he knew that Hogan
was right. He *was* always talking about joining the
army, about getting into the fighting and getting even.
But he never did anything about it. And now when
he might have a chance to do something . . . "I'm no
coward," he said defensively.

"Then prove it," said Hogan. "The least you could
do is go up and talk to that captain."

"Well . . . maybe I could do that," said Joshua.
"Just talk to him."

"Yeah!" Hogan exclaimed. He grabbed Joshua's
books and hustled him up the steps and into the
courthouse.

The lobby was a long passageway that led from the
front door of the building to the main courtroom in
the back. A small table had been set up along the
right-hand wall, behind which sat the captain. A re-
cruitment poster showing a handsome cavalryman
on his steed was attached to the front of the table.
Joshua left Hogan at the door and moved as casually
as he could down the hall. When he was opposite the
recruiting table, he stopped and pretended to admire
the poster.

"Colonel Wharton's Light Cavalry, son," said the
captain. "Finest cavalry in the field."

Joshua's throat was as dry as dust. He could not believe what he was doing. "Yes. Yes, sir," he managed
to say.

"Thinking of joining up?"

Joshua stared blankly at the captain and shrugged. "Dunno. How old do you have to be?"

"Eighteen."

"Ohhh," said Joshua. "Eighteen."

"How old are you?"

"'Bout sixteen," he stammered.

"You look a mite younger than that," the officer said. "What year were you born?"

Joshua had not expected the question and did some frantic computations in his head.

"Eighteen forty . . . forty-six. No, forty-nine, I think it was."

The officer smiled and his voice softened. "How old are you really, son?"

"Thirteen. In June."

"Well, you're a big fellow for your age. But you're a little young for us. If you were sixteen or seventeen, we might wink at it, but Colonel Wharton is pretty strict about his age requirement."

"Oh," said Joshua lamely. But inside he felt as if a huge cannonball had been lifted from his chest.

"What's your name?"

"Joshua. Joshua Loring."

"Well, Joshua Loring, do you have any older brothers who might be interested in signing up?"

"No, it's just me and my ma. My pa was a soldier, but he got killed at Fredericksburg."

The officer scratched his bearded chin and looked thoughtfully at Joshua. "I'll tell you what I'm going to do, young man. I'm going to write your name on this piece of paper here, and if we ever change our age policy, I'll let you know. You'll be the first one we contact. Fair enough?"

"Yes, sir."

As the officer scribbled a notation on his paper, Joshua glanced over at Hogan, who was still standing near the door. Hogan's face gaped in disbelief. He thinks I've really enlisted, Joshua thought, beginning to smile.

When the officer finished making his notation, he looked up. "Now, until you're old enough, I suggest you stay with your ma and help her as much as you can."

"Yes, sir," said Joshua, beginning to inch away from the table.

"Wait," the officer ordered. "Because you were my only customer today, I'd like to give you a small bounty." He reached into his pocket and slapped a pair of shiny two-cent pieces on the table. "So why don't you take this and go buy yourself some candy. And make sure you get some for your friend," he said, nodding toward Hogan.

Joshua thanked the officer and hurried down the corridor. "Let's go," he said, as he passed Hogan. Hogan needed no encouragement. He went after his friend like a dog chasing a stick. "You did it!" he gasped. "You really joined up!"

"Yup," said Joshua nonchalantly, "I'm gonna be a cavalryman."

"Unbelievable," Hogan blurted, slapping his friend on the back. "Just unbelievable." Then he added quickly, "Hey, Josh, did you think what your ma's gonna say?"

"Doesn't matter. There's nothing she can do now. The captain already made up the papers."

"She's gonna be real mad, Josh."

"You were the one who kept saying enlist, enlist," Joshua said, trying not to laugh.

"Yeah, but I never thought you really would."

Joshua shrugged. "You were wrong."

"What did he give you?" Hogan pressed.

"Money."

"Money! How much?"

"Enough. He said it was an advance on my bounty."

"I don't believe it," Hogan muttered again. "Was it a gold piece? C'mon, Josh, show me!"

Joshua bit his tongue and pulled the two-cent pieces from his pocket.

"Four cents?" asked Hogan incredulously. "He only gave you four cents for your bounty?" Joshua could contain himself no longer and burst out laughing. Hogan looked quizzically at his friend. "What's so funny?" he demanded.

Joshua was unable to answer through his laughter, and his eyes began to water. Hogan watched his friend for a moment. "What's so funny?" he repeated, choking back a laugh of his own.

Joshua pressed his lips together, trying to regain his composure. "I didn't enlist," he said at last. "He told me I was too young and gave me some money for candy."

Hogan shot Joshua the most disgusted look he could manage. "I knew you was lyin'," he blurted. "I was just playin' along."

Joshua laughed again. "You did not. You thought I got a four-cent bounty! Four cents!" He grabbed Hogan by the shoulders and swung him around so that they were both facing Harrison's. "Come on," he said, "I'll treat you to some vanilla chocolate."

Chapter Fourteen

oshua looked at the blank paper in front of him. His second letter to John Meadows was proving to be almost as difficult to write as his first. He had read the young soldier's letter so many times the paper had almost fallen to pieces. But the more he looked at it, the more confused he became. Why would John Meadows want to know about snowball fights? he wondered. And why would he possibly care about fishing when he was locked away in prison?

Each time Joshua put his pen to the paper, he found himself unable to scratch out a single word. Finally he threw his pen down and pushed himself away from his desk. He wandered downstairs to the kitchen.

"Morning," said Mrs. Loring without looking up from her ledger book.

"Morning."

"Sleep well?"

"Pretty good. I've been up for a while."

Joshua drifted toward the stove, where a pan of cornbread was cooling. He dipped his head over the bread and breathed in its sweet fragrance. "I'm having trouble writing to John Meadows," he said as he broke a small piece from the corner of the loaf and popped it into his mouth.

Mrs. Loring looked up.

"I just don't understand him, Ma. He wants to write about . . . about regular things."

"What do you mean?"

"You know . . . snowball fights and fishing. Things like that. He didn't ask anything 'bout the war. It just doesn't make sense, him being a soldier and all. Why would he care about those other things?"

Mrs. Loring put down her pen. "Well, it seems to me that he's a boy first and a soldier second. Just because you put on a uniform doesn't mean you stop thinking about the things you like. Your pa sure didn't. Did you ever think that this boy might be trying to dwell on happy things? Trying to put the war out of his mind?"

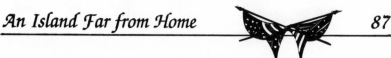

Joshua had not thought of that before. Maybe John Meadows was simply trying to forget where he was. Trying to escape from George's Island in his mind. "So you think he really wants to know about those things?"

"Yes," said Mrs. Loring. "Yes, I do."

Joshua stole another piece of cornbread and returned to his room. He had a better idea now of what he would say.

> *Dear Joh—*

Joshua's hand froze on the paper. He had made the same mistake in this letter that he had in his first. He considered starting anew but decided against it.

> *Dear John Meadows,*
> *I got your letter a little while ago. In the winter we have good snowball fights all the time. I go up to the woods with my friends and we make forts and have battles.*

As Joshua wrote, the words began to flow more easily.

> *I go to grammar school. My teacher is Mr. Rawson. We have a whole pile of diffrent lessons but my favourite is history. My best friend is named Tom Hogan, but everyone just calls him Hogan. We like to go fishing in*

*Latten's pond. We usually don't catch much
but sometimes we get bass or perch. I don't
have a pet right now but we used to have a
dog named Ginger.*

*What is it like in Alabama? Do you like
fishing? Do you ever get any snow?*

Joshua paused and wondered how he should sign
the letter. He felt awkward simply writing his name.
That was not the way letters were supposed to end. At
the same time, he didn't want to sound *too* friendly.
That wouldn't be right either. After thinking it over,
he decided that "sincerely" would be best and signed
his name.

Joshua read over the letter. It was not perfect, but
he was satisfied.

He didn't have to wait long for a reply. "Master Loring! Master Loring!" a muffled voice called as Joshua
passed the post office. Joshua stopped short and peered
through the window into the dimly lit building. Mr.
Tuttle, the postmaster, was standing behind the enormous counter, beckoning him to enter.

"You want me, Mr. Tuttle?"

The postmaster put down a stack of envelopes.
"You have a letter, lad."

"I do?" asked Joshua.

Mr. Tuttle moved to the side of the counter and

searched methodically through the cubbyholes that held the morning mail. "Here it is!" he said.

Joshua's pulse quickened as he took the letter. He had seen the handwriting before. "Thanks," he said, pushing the letter deep into his coat pocket. As soon as he stepped onto the sidewalk, he checked to see if any of his friends were in the square. When he was sure that no one would see him, he plopped down on the cold granite steps of the courthouse, tore open the envelope, and pulled out a piece of heavy paper.

Dear Joshua,

Joshua smiled. John Meadows must have made the same mistake.

> *I got your letter today. I never seen much snow before I got here! During our free time we have good snow battles with the guards. Once we played a game called football in the snow too. I think it's fun but I wish the winter was a mite warmer. My gloves got worn out and my hands get powerful cold. In Mobile, it's pretty much warm most of the time. I live in a cottage near the Fire Company house. It's painted white and we got all kinds of flowers and bushes in the yard. Specially azalyas. I miss it real bad.*
> *Sometimes I fish in the bay, but there are*

cricks nearby too. We get trout, sheephead and white perch.

Yours truely,
John Meadows

Joshua continued to stare at the letter. Mobile didn't sound like a bad place, he thought, and the young Rebel liked to do some of the same things he did. He tucked the letter into his pocket, stood up, and walked toward his house. He wanted to finish his chores and his schoolwork. But most of all, he wanted to write back to John Meadows.

Chapter Fifteen

oshua pressed his shoulder against the door to the woodshed until he heard the latch click. His arms were piled high with logs and kindling, and he walked carefully over the patches of ice that dotted the back walkway to his house. The morning air was dry and cold, like the inside of an ice house. Joshua's breath swirled about him in small clouds. "It's freezin' out," he said as he stumbled through the doorway into the warmth of the kitchen.

"I was remarking to Mrs. Nelson the other day," said Mrs. Loring, "that this was one of the coldest winters I could remember. I'll be so happy when the warm weather comes."

"Sure, Ma," Joshua joked, "and *then* you'll be so happy when the cold weather comes."

Joshua put the wood in a large basket in the parlor and laid his coat and mittens by the fireplace to warm. "We have anything hot to drink?" he called as he squatted down and held his hands, palms up, near the flames. He could feel the heat work its way through his fingers and up his arms.

After several minutes Mrs. Loring emerged from the kitchen, carrying a steaming cup. "Drink this slowly," she warned. "It's very hot."

Joshua took a sip of tea and let it trickle down his throat. "Must be real cold on George's Island."

"Yes, Robert said it's been bitter there."

"The Rebs got fireplaces, don't they?"

"Oh, I'm sure they do. They'd freeze without them. Robert wouldn't allow that."

That was true, Joshua thought. Uncle Robert would never let the prisoners suffer. He held the cup near his cheek and let its warmth seep into his face. "They have winter coats?" he asked.

"The prisoners?"

"Yeah."

"Well, I . . . I think so. I know that there are some groups in Boston that send clothing and supplies to the island."

Joshua looked at his mother in astonishment. "They're allowed to do that?"

"Why, yes, at least they were at one time." Mrs. Loring looked at the clock on the parlor wall. "Have you finished your lessons?"

"Not all of them," Joshua mumbled, knowing full well that he had not even started.

"Well, you'd better finish today. Tomorrow's church," said Mrs. Loring as she disappeared into the kitchen.

Joshua pulled himself away from the hearth and climbed the stairs to his room, where a copy of *Peterson's Grammar* awaited him. He sank reluctantly into his chair and opened the book to the chapter entitled "Adjectives." Boring, he thought. "An adjective is a word used to qualify a noun," he read, although he was not certain what that meant. Beneath the definition was a long, alphabetized list of examples. "Abrupt. Adept. Beautiful. Better. Big. Bold. Buttery. Certain. Cold." His eyes stopped and lingered on the word *cold*. He reached for the white envelope, opened it, and began to read. One line stood apart from the others. "My gloves got worn out and my hands get powerful cold." Joshua sat back in his chair and closed his eyes. He could see a young Rebel soldier, a faceless soldier, standing alone and shivering on a windswept island.

He closed his grammar book and crept downstairs. He could hear his mother in the kitchen humming, her

voice rising and falling in melodic waves. He tiptoed
across the parlor to the fireplace, where he had left his
mittens—the pair his mother had given him at Christmas. They were dry and warm now, and he stuffed
them beneath his shirt.

When he returned to his room, he removed the mittens and placed them on his bed. Then he sat at his
desk and dashed off a short note.

> *Dear John,*
> *Hope these fit. You can keep them. Don't*
> *worry. I have another pair.*
> > *Sincerely,*
> > *Joshua*

He rummaged through his room until he found a
piece of heavy paper and some string. He folded the
note and placed it in one of the mittens and then
wrapped and tied them securely. He addressed the
package to: Private John Meadows, Prisoner, Fort
Warren, George's Island, Massachusetts. With luck
Uncle Robert would never find out that he had given
his new mittens away.

Joshua dug his old mittens from the bottom of
his dresser drawer and shoved them into one side of
his shirt. Into the other side he tucked the package
for John. He took a deep breath and descended the
stairs. "Ma, I'm going to the square," he yelled. "You
need anything at the store?"

Mrs. Loring poked her head into the parlor. "Why are you going to the square?" she asked.

"To see Hogan."

"What about your lessons?"

"Finished 'em." Joshua crossed his arms tightly over his stomach so that his mother would not detect the bulge under his shirt.

"You finished already? You haven't been upstairs more than twenty minutes."

"I finished," Joshua said, shrugging.

Mrs. Loring turned but then stopped. "Be back no later than five."

"Yes, ma'am."

Joshua struggled into his coat, tugged his cap down to his brow, and walked out onto the front porch. He was greeted by a gust of wind that sent a shiver coursing through him. He thrust his bare hands into his pockets and scurried down the front walk. When he reached the safety of the road, he took his old mittens from his shirt and slipped them onto his hands. He had made it!

Chapter Sixteen

ogan traced the words with his finger as he read aloud: "'Fondly do we hope—fer . . . fervently do we pray—that this mighty sc . . . scourge of war may speedily pass away.'"

Joshua peered over his friend's shoulder and strained to see the tiny print of the clipping on the door of the telegraph office. Abraham Lincoln's second inaugural address, given in Washington on March 4, had traveled the wires to Tilton.

"Sounds like Old Abe wants the war to end," said Hogan.

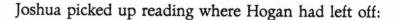

Joshua picked up reading where Hogan had left off:

> *Yet, if God wills that it continue, until all the wealth piled by the bond-man's two hundred and fifty years of unre . . . unrequited toil shall be sunk, and until every drop of blood drawn with the lash, shall be paid by another drawn with the sword, as was said three thousand years ago, so still it must be said "the judgments of the Lord, are true and righteous altogether."*

"What's that all mean?" Hogan asked.

Joshua considered the president's words. "I think it means that we'll keep fighting until all the slaves are free and the South gives up."

"Well, we *should* keep fightin'," said Hogan emphatically. "The South was the one who fired at Fort Sumter first. They were the ones who started the whole thing. I just never understood that."

There were things Joshua did not understand either. As the stack of letters on his desk grew higher, questions nagged at him like mosquitoes on a hot summer's night. What was John fighting for? And why would a boy so much like himself join the Rebel army? Maybe it was about time he asked John those very questions. Maybe it was about time they stopped pretending that the war didn't exist.

"Listen to this," said Hogan.

With malice toward none; with charity for all; with firmness in the right, as God gives us to see the right, let us strive on to finish the work we are in; to bind up the nation's wounds; to care for him who shall have borne the battle, and for his widow, and his orphan—to do all which may achieve and cherish a just, and a lasting peace, among ourselves, and with all nations.

Hogan furrowed his brow. "I'm not sure what Old Abe's sayin', but if he wants to win first and then make peace, I'm all for it."

It was the easiest letter Joshua had written to John. And the hardest. He knew exactly what he had to say, and the words streamed from his pen. Yet as he wrote, Joshua feared that his questions might make John angry and that this letter might be his last.

Dear John,
I'm writing because there's something that's been bothering me. I know all about you from your letters, but you never say anything about why your fighting us. I don't understand it. Is it because you have slaves or you wanted to be with your friends or do you just hate us? Don't you care about your country any more?

I hope this letter doesn't get you all riled up but it's just something I have to know.
Sincerely,
Joshua

John's reply arrived the following week.

Dear Joshua,

I just got your letter. You asked me why I decided to fight. Well, I'll tell you. It's sure not because I hate you. I'm fighting because Lincoln and the Yankees invaded our land and thought they could do whatever they wanted to us even though we're our own state. I'm fighting to protect my folks so we can go on living the way we been living. You'd do the same if we invaded your town.

My Pa don't own slaves and neither do a lot of men in my regiment. But I know some people who do. They aren't bad folk. Having slaves is the way things always been. George Washington hisself owned slaves. That's how farms and plantations work. Without slaves therd be no cotton or tobacco. And the whole country would fall apart. I know we don't see eye to eye on these things but I got real good cause for fighting.

Yours truely,
John

*By the way, I aint all angered up. I hope
you keep writing.*

Joshua folded the letter and put it back in its envelope. John's got it all wrong, he thought. The
North's not invading the South. It's just trying to
keep the country together, like Lincoln said, and make
the slaves free. That's all. But John's letter got Joshua
thinking. What if Rebel troops had marched north
and tried to bring Massachusetts within the Confederacy? What if they had demanded that he change his
way of life? How would he feel? What would he do?
Maybe if he and John could meet face to face and talk
it out, everything would make more sense. Maybe
that's what the president meant when he said: With
malice toward none, let us strive to bind up the nation's wounds.

Chapter Seventeen

ou're going to split your head, Josh. One of these days you'll go right over backward in that chair and split your head."

Joshua eased his chair down until its front legs were planted firmly on the floor. "No I won't," he mumbled. "I've been doin' this forever, and I've never gone over."

"Well, I don't like it," said Mrs. Loring, "so don't do it."

When his mother turned away, Joshua pressed his feet against the floor and leaned back until the front legs of his chair were only a hair's breadth off the ground. He watched as his mother moved from chair to table to cabinet to chair, her duster gliding faster than a bird in flight. When Mrs. Loring reached the fireplace, she paused to look at a silver-framed photograph on the mantel. A handsome face, tinted brown, stared out from behind a piece of protective glass.

"Do you still miss Pa as much?" Joshua asked.

"Yes," said Mrs. Loring, gazing at the picture.

"Me too."

"Sometimes I think I miss him more as time goes on. Even the little things."

"Like what, Ma?"

"Well . . . when we went to church, your father used to take my hand during the sermon. I miss that. And I miss the evenings when we used to read aloud to each other." She paused. "And I wish he were here for you."

Joshua looked back at the photograph. His eyes lingered on his father's. "Did Pa ever have any friends from the South?" he asked.

"Yes, he did," said Mrs. Loring. "When he was at Harvard College, he had a good friend from Virginia. Stephen Sturges was his name. I knew him too."

"Was he a Reb?"

"Not back then. That was years before the war . . . before you were born." Mrs. Loring smiled. "He was a funny young fellow. He and your father were always up to some mischief."

"Like what?"

"Oh . . . different things."

"Come on, Ma, what?"

Mrs. Loring's face broke into a wide grin. "I shouldn't be telling you this," she said.

"Come on, Ma."

"Well, both your father and Stephen spoke French well, and sometimes they would go to parties and pretend that they were French artists visiting Boston. They put on quite an act and had everyone fooled."

"How do you know they did that?"

Mrs. Loring's smile dissolved into sadness. "Because that's how we met. At one of those parties."

Joshua's mouth fell open. "You thought Pa was a famous French painter?" he blurted.

Mrs. Loring blushed, and her smile returned. "The first time I met him, yes."

"Boy, did he hoodwink you, Ma!" said Joshua, laughing. "What happened to Stephen?"

"He moved to Richmond after graduation. We used to hear from him from time to time. But then," she said, her voice trailing off, "the war came. And that was that."

Joshua's face grew serious. "Do you think if Pa was alive, he'd still be friends with him?"

"Yes," said Mrs. Loring, "I can't imagine them being enemies."

Joshua nodded. "And I bet they'd be good friends,"

he added.

"Speaking of friends, what have you heard from John?"

Joshua was caught off guard. "How come you called him my friend?"

"Well, you two have been writing to each other for quite a while now. I just supposed that he might be a friend."

"Maybe," said Joshua cautiously.

Mrs. Loring resumed her cleaning, her duster touching everything in her path. "What have you two been writing about?"

"Different things. He tells me a lot, and I tell him a lot."

"I see."

Joshua got up from his chair and lifted a heavy vase so his mother could dust beneath it. "What's quoits?" he asked suddenly.

"Quoits?"

"John says they play it at the fort."

"It's a game where you try to throw a ring around a peg. You must have played it before."

"I don't remember," said Joshua.

"What else does he do at the fort?"

"Works at the bakery."

"Is he a baker?"

"No, a baker's helper. He cleans the ovens and delivers bread to the other prisoners. And he helps make

something called ashcake that doesn't taste so good."

"That sounds like an important job."

"It is." Joshua's voice grew animated as he revealed more from John's letters. "He says that after dinner's the best time. They sing. And tell stories. And play checkers. And that's when he writes to me. Sometimes the prisoners and guards even have contests to see who can sing the loudest. The guards sing 'John Brown's Body' and the Rebs sing 'Dixie.' He says most of the guards treat them pretty good." Joshua forced a smile. "I still think John's kinda lonely. He doesn't get any other letters. He doesn't even know where his folks are now."

"That's very sad," said Mrs. Loring. "Prison is not a decent place for a young boy to be. Even a good prison."

"Maybe I could visit him sometime," Joshua suggested offhandedly. He waited for his mother's reaction.

Mrs. Loring stopped her dusting. "I don't know if that's possible, Josh."

"Just for a little while. John says he'd like to meet me too."

"It's not up to me. You'll have to ask Robert. But I wouldn't set my hopes on it. Fort Warren is a military camp, and those Rebels are still enemy soldiers."

"But John isn't the enemy. He's—"

"I know, Josh, I know," Mrs. Loring interrupted. "All I'm saying is don't get your hopes up."

"I can ask Uncle Robert, though, right?"

"Yes, you may. In fact, he plans to visit next week."

The prospect of seeing John set Joshua's mind whirling. He rushed up the stairs to his room and grabbed his pen.

> *Dear John,*
>
> *I just wanted to write and say that I'm asking my uncle if I can go to the island sometime and see you. That would be great. And we could talk about things too. I can't remember playing quoits before but you could teach me. It sounds like fun.*
>
>

Your friend,
Joshua
>

Joshua looked at how he had signed the letter. His mother was right. He and John *were* friends.

Chapter
Eighteen

L ate March brought the first birds of spring to Tilton. They arrived in clusters and settled in the treetops. For the first time in months, the air was filled with the sounds of their songs. Joshua and Hogan picked their way along the wooded path that led to Latten's Pond. The earth had turned to a muddy ooze, forcing the boys to hug the side of the trail.

"Birds are startin' to sing," Joshua observed, pausing to listen to the *konk-la-ree* of a red-winged blackbird.

"Ya know," said Hogan pensively, "most of these birds been down south. I bet some even flew over the

Reb armies. You wonder what they seen."

"Too bad we can't turn 'em into spies, like Lincoln's secret agents."

The boys plodded ahead through the heavy vegetation alongside the trail. "Hey," said Hogan, "we get to write to your uncle soon."

"Yup," Joshua answered matter-of-factly.

"You don't sound too excited 'bout it."

"Yeah, I am. I was just thinking about something else."

"You're lucky you'll get to make a pick. The war's gonna end real soon. That's what everyone's sayin'. The whole Reb army's on the run now."

Joshua bobbed his head in agreement. The Confederacy seemed to be gasping its last breath.

The boys emerged from the woods at the steep bank of the pond. The sun was dazzlingly bright, and for an instant they were blinded by the light reflecting off the mirrorlike ice.

"Think it's safe to walk on?" Joshua asked. "There's no one out there."

Hogan scurried down the bank and picked up a rock. He drew back his arm and threw it far out over the ice. It landed with a dull thud and skidded across the surface, raising a thin spray of water. "It's safe," he pronounced. "If it was thin, it woulda gone through. Besides," he added, "it was so cold this winter, the ice'll be around till July."

Joshua was not quite so sure. He searched the ground until he found a larger rock and hurled it onto the ice to test it for himself. As with Hogan's, the rock landed with a thud and skidded toward the center of the pond. "I guess it's all right," he said, climbing down the bank to where Hogan was standing. "You want me to try it?"

"Nah, I'll do it," said Hogan. "I'm lighter than you." He stepped gingerly onto the ice and began to prod the surface with his boot.

"Looks like it's startin' to melt a little," Joshua cautioned.

"Nah, it's still real hard."

Hogan made his way further out onto the ice, testing it as he went. Tap. Tap. Tap. Step. Tap. Tap. Tap. Step. When he was about twenty-five feet from the bank, he turned and motioned to Joshua. "Come on! Don't be afraid!"

Joshua stepped onto the ice. It was wet and slippery, but it held his weight. When he was convinced that it would not give way, he slid carefully over to Hogan.

"I told ya, it's thick," Hogan repeated.

Joshua removed a small hatchet from his belt, bent over, and began to strike the ice gently. With each blow, small pieces of frozen ice like tiny diamonds flew through the air. After several moments he stopped. "Doesn't feel right," he said.

"What d'ya mean?"

"Usually when it's frozen real good, you can feel the vibrations go all the way up your arm when you hit it. This doesn't feel that way."

"Let *me* see."   Hogan grabbed the hatchet and squatted where Joshua had begun to chip away the ice. He lifted the hatchet high above his head and brought it down with a crash. The ice groaned.

Joshua glared at Hogan. "You're being stupid," he said angrily. "I'm going back." He turned and walked slowly toward the pond's muddy bank.

"Come on back, Josh! Don't be yella! It's at least three or four inches," Hogan shouted.

Joshua did not look back until his feet touched solid ground.   Then he turned and watched his friend whack stubbornly at the ice.

"I'm almost through!" Hogan yelled.

"Come on!" Joshua implored.   "Don't be a fool!"

Over the groaning and creaking of the ice, a new sound, a sharp snapping noise, filled the air. Hogan glanced up for a split second, fear etched in his eyes.

"Get off!" Joshua screamed.

Hogan tried to stand, but it was too late. The ice buckled, and Joshua watched in horror as his friend disappeared beneath the frigid waters of the pond. A horrible silence followed. Joshua knew he had to do something, and do it quickly, but his legs were cold and lifeless. He could only stare transfixed at the spot

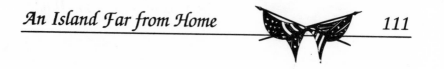

where Hogan had been seconds before.

Suddenly Hogan's head and arms broke the surface of the water, and he thrashed wildly, gulping for air and clawing at the jagged shards of ice that surrounded the hole. But as desperately as he tried, the slippery surface would not take his hold, and he was pulled back into the black void.

He's alive! Joshua thought. He's alive! It was as if a magician had snapped his fingers and released him from a deep trance. He turned quickly and scanned the bank until he spotted a fallen branch. He ran to it and lugged it back to where he had been standing. Then he crawled onto the ice, lay down flat on his stomach, and spread his weight. He thrust the branch out in front of him. "Please, dear Lord," he whispered as he worked his way across the ice, "please make him come up."

Joshua pushed the branch forward some twenty feet until it spanned the blackened hole. "Please, dear Lord . . . please," he prayed once more. Then, as if in answer to his prayer, Hogan again broke the surface of the water. Joshua jiggled the branch back and forth. "Grab it!" he screamed. "Grab it!"

Hogan's hand flailed above the hole until it found the branch. Then his fingers tightened like a vise around it.

Joshua summoned all the strength he possessed and pulled back on the branch. Never in his life had he strained so hard. His veins bulged, and his muscles felt as if they would explode. Slowly, ever so slowly, he lifted Hogan from his icy pit and dragged him to the safety of the shore.

"You all right?" Joshua gasped.

Hogan nodded feebly. He slumped in a shivering heap against the muddy bank. Joshua huddled next to his friend. Now that they were safe, he realized that he too was cold and wet—and utterly exhausted.

"Josh," Hogan said weakly, "that was pretty dumb, huh?"

"Yeah, real dumb."

"We're still friends, though, right?"

"Yeah," Joshua answered through chattering teeth, "friends forever."

Chapter Nineteen

*T*he footsteps on the stairs grew louder and louder. Joshua could tell immediately that more than one person was coming. He shifted himself in his bed and propped up his pillows behind him. There was a knock on the door, and his mother poked her head into the room. "Josh, you have a visitor."

"Who is it?"

A large hand appeared and pushed the door ajar. "What do you mean, who is it?" a voice thundered from the hallway. "Whom were you expecting—the Queen of England?" Uncle Robert charged through

the door, trailed by Mrs. Loring. "So this is the sick room, is it?" he said, glancing about.

"Yeah," said Joshua sheepishly.

"How are you feeling?"

"Pretty good. My head's still sorta stuffed up."

"A little castor oil and tincture of iron, and you'll be back on your feet in no time. And your friend Hogan, how is he?"

"Good."

"He didn't even catch a sniffle," said Mrs. Loring, shaking her head. "He's the one who falls through the ice, and it's Josh who gets a fearful cold."

"Hmmm," said Uncle Robert, "that's usually the way. Now Catherine," he said, turning to his sister, "what do you say you give us men a few minutes alone here."

Mrs. Loring eyed her brother warily. "What do you have up your sleeve? Secrets?"

"Top secrets," Robert responded in mock serious-ness. "From Lincoln himself."

"Don't you get him excited, Robert, or he'll start coughing again."

"Don't worry, I'll be on my best behavior."

When Mrs. Loring had gone, Uncle Robert sat down at the foot of Joshua's bed. "I have a little something for you," he said, looking back at the door. "I don't know whether you're supposed to have it or not." Robert reached into his pocket and pulled out a bag of hard candies.

Joshua stared greedily at the small nuggets. For the past several days, his mother had given him nothing but soups and medicines. His stomach cried for sweets. "Thanks, he whispered, "I'll hide 'em." He reached over and put the candy in the top drawer of his night table.

"So," said Robert, "are you going back to school soon?"

"Monday, I think."

"That's good. Very good." Uncle Robert cleared his throat. "I . . . ah . . . heard about what you did at the pond, Josh. That took a great deal of courage. In the army they give medals for deeds that aren't nearly as brave. I just want you to know how proud I am of you."

"It wasn't much," Joshua said, but inside he was elated. Uncle Robert was a genuine war hero. There was no man alive he admired more. Not Grant. Not Sherman. Not even Old Abe himself. And now to have Robert say that he was proud of him. Well, that was as good as any medal.

Robert stood up and walked over to his nephew's desk. "Are these from John Meadows?" he asked, pointing to a neatly piled stack of envelopes.

"Yeah, we've been writin' a lot."

"I can see that."

"Do you ever . . . Do you ever talk to him?"

"From time to time, yes."

"About what?"

"Well, we talk about a lot of things. The prison.
The war. Fishing. And we've talked about you."

Joshua sat up, eager to hear more. "What does he
want to know about me?"

"He says he's learned a lot about you from your
letters. But he wanted to know what you looked
like. Apparently you two have never exchanged
descriptions."

"And?" Joshua asked expectantly.

"Well, I told him that the men in our family were
the handsomest fellows in Massachusetts."

Joshua stifled a laugh. "What did you *really* say?"

"I said that you were a big, strong, strapping young
man with auburn hair and blue eyes."

"He doesn't think I'm a bookworm 'cuz I write so
much, does he?"

"No. I gather he writes as much as you do. And I
think your letters are very important to him. They
make him feel like the boy he was before the war."

Joshua leaned his head back until it touched the
thick oak headboard, and stared at the ceiling. "I bet
I know what John looks like," he said. "I bet he's big.
Like me. And he's got black hair. And his front tooth
is chipped from a battle."

Uncle Robert smiled. "You're close. Except his hair
is blond and his teeth are full and straight."

Joshua reached for a handkerchief and wiped his

nose. "You know what's strange, I don't even think of him as a Reb anymore. I kinda think of him like Hogan. Isn't that odd?"

Uncle Robert shook his head. "Not really. I've met many a prisoner at the fort whom I suspect I'd be friends with in different circumstances."

"What's going to happen to John when the war ends?"

"He'll be released or exchanged for Union prisoners. And put on a boat and sent back south. He should be one of the first to leave, because of his age."

"Will he be hurt?"

"No, he'll be fine. I'll see to that."

All the talking had started Joshua coughing again.

"I'd better go now," Robert whispered, "before your mother scolds me for interfering with your rest." He gripped his nephew's hand. "Now you stay in bed and do what your ma says to get well. Fair enough?"

"Yeah."

Robert turned and walked toward the door.

"Uncle Robert?" Joshua called. Robert stopped and swung around. "Don't go yet. There's somethin' I need to ask." Joshua struggled to find the right words. "Well, I was just sorta wonderin' . . . if maybe . . . there's some way I could see John. I'd really like to meet him."

"Josh," said Robert, "there's nothing I'd rather see than you two boys getting together. I know it would mean a lot to both of you. And you've been more of a friend to John than I think you realize." Joshua could sense his uncle's next words. "But I'm sorry. Unless there is special authorization from Washington, the regulations only allow soldiers on the island. That's one of the rules we have to follow. It would be too dangerous if just anyone could walk around out there."

"Oh," Joshua sighed.

Robert could see the disappointment in his nephew's face. "I'm sorry," he said again. He opened the door and began to step out. Then he stopped and, in a voice Joshua could barely hear, said, "By the way, John mentioned the mittens you sent him a while back."

Joshua felt his cheeks flush.

"You know," his uncle whispered, glancing toward the stairs, "they looked a lot like the ones you got last Christmas."

"I told Ma I lost 'em."

"Your secret's safe with me."

When Robert had gone, Joshua reached into his night table and took a piece of hard candy. The sweet flavor soothed his scratchy throat but not his disappointment. He played Robert's words over and over in his mind. If only his uncle had said "Maybe" or "Wait and see." Then there would have been some hope that he could meet John. But Robert's words were as clear as clear could be. Only soldiers were allowed on the island. Only soldiers.

Chapter Twenty

r. Rawson tapped his pointer against the side of his desk. "May I have quiet?" he asked. As the class grew silent, he ambled across the front of the room to the window that overlooked the schoolyard. "I know it is difficult to be attentive during the first warm days of spring," he said, gazing through the freshly cleaned panes of glass, "but we must maintain our discipline. Summer will be here soon enough, and then you may become idlers." Mr. Rawson moved back to the center of the room and locked his eyes on Joshua.

Joshua shifted uneasily in his seat, trying to untangle

the knot that had formed in his stomach.

"I believe it is Master Loring's turn to provide us with a name for our letter-writing campaign."

"Yes, sir," said Joshua.

"As all of you are probably aware," Mr. Rawson continued, "this may be the last batch of letters we send. The Army of Northern Virginia is almost broken, and the newspapers say that Richmond and Petersburg will fall soon. I think our brave young men and women will be returning home before long, so I suggest that we write our letters most expeditiously. Are you ready, Master Loring?"

"Yes," Joshua replied, although his body said no. He eased himself from behind his desk and found his footing. After what seemed an eternity, he made it to the front of the room. "I would like . . . ," he said, swallowing hard, "for everyone to write . . ." He paused and looked up at his classmates. It was now or never, he thought. "I would like . . . ," he began again, "for the class to write to a soldier at Fort Warren, on George's Island. He's a private who was in the Battle of Mobile Bay." Joshua shot a glance at Hogan. "He's only a little older than me," Joshua continued, "and his name's John Meadows."

"John Meadows?!" Hogan blurted. "What about your uncle?"

"Master Hogan," said Mr. Rawson, "we do not talk out of turn." Then he turned to Joshua. "Thank you

very much, Master Loring. We will send Private
Meadows his letters as quickly as possible."

Joshua started to return to his seat but stopped
midway down the aisle. "There's something else, sir."

"Yes?"

Joshua hesitated. He could feel a huge lump forming in his throat.

"Yes, what is it?" asked Mr. Rawson impatiently.

"He's a . . ."

"Yes?"

"He's a . . . prisoner at the fort."

Joshua forced himself to look at Hogan. His friend's
face was frozen in shock. And there was a collective
gasp from the other students in the class.

"I ain't writin' no Reb!" Tim Rodgers hooted.

"I ain't either!" shouted a girl with black curls.

"Reb-lover!"

Joshua's face turned the color of blood, as much
from anger as from embarrassment.

Mr. Rawson slammed his pointer against his desk
so hard it sounded like the report of a cannon.
"Quiet!" he ordered. "I'll have none of this in my
schoolroom!" He turned to Joshua. "This presents
somewhat of a problem, Master Loring. I am sure that
there are scholars here who are opposed to writing to a
Confederate soldier. Very much opposed."

"He's a traitor!" Tim Rodgers screeched.

"You be quiet!" Mr. Rawson commanded, pointing

his huge stick in Tim's direction. Then, in a low voice, he said, "Master Loring, perhaps you could make another choice, one that would be more acceptable."

Joshua shook his head. "No, sir. I mean to keep John Meadows as my choice."

"Why, Joshua? What is it about this boy that made you choose him?"

"I'm . . . I'm not sure," Joshua stammered. "I think he's lonely and . . . he's a lot like us, you know. He likes the same things we do, and he's afraid of the same things. He's a Reb 'cause he was born in Alabama. If we were born there, we'd probably be Rebs, too." Joshua fought the tears that welled up in his eyes. "My pa helped Reb soldiers who got wounded, and he was no traitor. He did it because it was the right thing to do. And writing John is the right thing to do. Even my uncle says so."

A strange quiet settled over the room. Mr. Rawson rubbed his thick chin and looked at his young charge. "Master Loring has made a good point," he said after a time. "I will not require anyone in the class to write to Private Meadows, but those of you who wish to may do so. I think it's something you should speak with your parents about."

Joshua returned quietly to his seat.

"I don't believe it," Hogan hissed. "What's wrong with you?"

"Nothing's wrong with me," Joshua whispered. "It

was just something I wanted to do."

Hogan shook his head in disgust and turned away. Joshua buried his head in a book and pretended to read, but his mind saw only the hateful stares of his classmates boring through him and branding him as a traitor. If only they knew John, he thought.

After school the class spilled onto the schoolyard. Joshua remained seated and watched as the room emptied. "Wanna go to the square?" he asked Hogan, who was busy strapping his books. Hogan did not answer. He did not even look up. He fastened the clip on his strap, slung his books over his shoulder, and stalked out the door.

Sadness flooded through Joshua. He knew he had made the right decision, but he never thought it would make him feel so utterly alone. As he gathered his books and started for the door, he was met by Mr. Rawson. "Joshua, I know that was a very difficult thing for you to do."

Joshua shrugged. He did not know what to say.

"There are certain qualities I admire in others," Mr. Rawson continued, "and one of them is the ability to do or say what they think is right, no matter what the consequences."

Joshua made a feeble attempt to smile. He knew Mr. Rawson was trying to make him feel better.

"Whether your friends agree with you or not, eventually most will come to respect your choice. You will see that."

Joshua nodded, but he was not convinced. He walked past Mr. Rawson and stepped out into the warm sunlight. He surveyed the schoolyard, hoping that Hogan had waited, but the only faces he saw belonged to Tim Rodgers and another boy whom he did not know.

Joshua hustled across the yard toward the square. The two boys followed behind him. "Hey, Loring! Where ya goin'?" Tim shouted.

"I bet I know where he's goin'," said the other boy. "He's goin' to help some Reb escape from prison! That right, Loring?"

"Yeah," said Tim, "he loves them Rebs." Joshua quickened his pace as the boys closed in. "And you know what he told us?" Tim sneered. "He said his pa was a traitor and a Reb-lover, too!"

As the words sunk in, Joshua felt something snap inside him. He flung his books to the ground and wheeled around so fast he startled the boys behind him. "Take that back!" he shouted furiously.

Tim looked at his friend and then at Joshua. "Why don't you try and make us? Or are you just plain yella?"

Joshua felt a rage he had never felt before. He bolted forward and brought Tim crashing to the ground with a sharp tackle. At the same time, he felt a stinging blow to his cheek as the other boy landed

a solid punch. He ducked his head low and began to shake Tim by the shoulders. "Take it back!" he screamed.

Another blow landed on Joshua's face with such force that he rolled off Tim and onto the ground. He could feel a thick stream of blood begin to flow from his nose. Sensing victory, Tim leaped to his feet and sent a strong kick to Joshua's stomach. Just as he was preparing to deliver another, a high-pitched shriek filled the air. A battle cry. The bullies froze, and Joshua lifted his head in the direction of the yell. There, no more than a hundred feet away, was Hogan, running full speed toward Joshua's tormentors and screaming, "Charrrrge!"

Tim and his companion exchanged nervous glances. "Come on," said Tim, "we beat up the traitor enough. Let's get outta here." He and the other boy fled across the road into the adjoining woods.

"You all right?" Hogan called as he drew near.

Joshua fumbled in his pocket for a handkerchief and wiped the blood from his nose and chin. "I think so."

"It wasn't a fair fight," Hogan offered. "That's why I did it." His voice was cold and unfeeling.

"Thanks anyway," Joshua said.

"We're even now, Josh, all even."

Joshua could tell by the look in Hogan's eyes that he had lost his best friend.

Chapter
Twenty-one

Joshua heard the bells first, a faint, distant pealing that spread through the still night and filtered into his home. "Ma, the church bells are ringing!" he yelled from the parlor.

Mrs. Loring appeared at the top of the stairwell and listened. "That's odd," she said, "all the Sunday services are over. I wonder if there's been a fire."

"Maybe," Joshua replied. "Or maybe there's been a big battle! Remember how they rang the bells after Atlanta. And after Gettysburg."

"Why don't you go to the square and see what's

happened," said Mrs. Loring.

Joshua needed no encouragement. He ran to the back room and threw on his boots and jacket. "I bet Grant and Lee had a battle!" he said excitedly as he raced past the stairwell and flew through the door.

"Come back as soon as you find out!" Mrs. Loring shouted after him. "And if there's a fire, stay away from it!"

Joshua sprinted down the front walkway and into the night. As the light from the spire of the church came into view, a horseman thundered toward him from the town. "What's going on?" Joshua called, moving to the side of the road as the rider drew near.

A middle-aged man wearing a floppy hat jerked the reins of his horse and came to a halt. "Almost didn't see ya there, boy."

"What's going on?" Joshua cried out again.

"Lee surrendered, son!" the man yelled. "And my boy'll be coming home!" He gave his horse a spur and took off down the road.

Joshua watched the rider disappear into the darkness. Could the horseman's words be true? It seemed that the country had been at war for as long as he could remember. Was it really over? Thoughts filled his mind. All the young men would be returning, and he would never be a soldier, would never fight in a great battle. Uncle Robert would be a lawyer again. And, he thought, John Meadows would be sent back to Alabama. He debated whether he should continue on into town or return home to tell his mother the news. But the bells answered the question for him. They beckoned him toward the square.

Tilton Square was in pandemonium when Joshua arrived. Horses and carriages clogged Main Street, and scores of people were converging on the courthouse. An enormous bonfire was blazing. The church bells were still ringing, horses were neighing, and townsfolk were cheering.

Joshua joined the joyous throng as it surged through the street. A podium had been erected near the top of the courthouse steps, and several men were gathered behind it. Joshua recognized one of them as Ezra Fields, Tilton's mayor.

"What's the news, Ezra?" a man shouted. "Is it official?"

"Yes, is it true?" several other men yelled out. The mayor approached the podium and raised his hand for silence. "I have news of the greatest importance," he announced, his voice rising with excitement. A hush settled over the crowd. "We have just received word over the telegraph that General Lee has surrendered his army to General Grant at a place called Appomattox Court House!"

The crowd let out a thunderous cheer. Emotions that had been building for four years erupted in their voices.

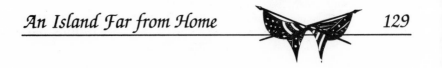

"Hurrah for General Grant!" Mayor Fields shouted. "And hurrah for his gallant soldiers!"

The crowd began to chant. "Hurrah for General Grant! Hurrah for the Union!" Joshua found himself swept away in the hysteria. He yelled and cheered until his throat was raw. We've done it, he thought. We've won! We've finally won!

After several minutes of celebration, the mayor again raised his hand for silence. "Now, the war's not officially over yet. Not as long as there are still Rebel armies in the field. But today's great events will cause the South to tumble like a house of cards in the wind." The mayor paused and looked out over the mass of townspeople assembled before him. "Tomorrow," he said in a voice that carried across the square, "is declared a day of jubilation! All schools are to be closed at noontime, and all citizens are invited to the square to celebrate the victory of our great armies! The hour of victory is upon us! Godspeed the return of our brave young men in uniform!" The crowd let out a roar of approval and clapped wildly.

Joshua felt lightheaded and unable to breathe. He broke away from the crowd, dropped down on the curb outside the barber shop, and filled his lungs with the fresh April air. As he surveyed the spectacle before him, his eyes were drawn to a small figure standing on the edge of the crowd. It was Hogan, cheering and waving his hands above his head. The boys had not

talked for almost a week now. And a week was too
long for Joshua. He pushed himself up from the curb
and retraced his steps across the square.

"I can't believe it's almost over," he said, sidling up
to the smaller boy.

Hogan stopped clapping and stared coldly at him.
"How come you're not with your Reb friend? Bet he's
not cheerin' now."

The words stung, but Joshua tried to ignore them.
"It's almost over, Hogan. He won't be a Reb anymore.
Everyone'll be the same."

"Yeah, sure, Josh, one minute they're Rebs and we're
tryin' to kill 'em, and the next minute they're our best
friends. You're crazy."

"Lee surrendered, Hogan. People are gonna have to
live together again."

Hogan shook his head in disgust and looked away,
but Joshua was not about to let him escape so easily.
He grabbed Hogan's shoulders and spun him so that
they faced each other. "I need your help," he said ur-
gently. "There's something important I need to do."

Joshua could tell from Hogan's expression that he
had kindled a spark of interest. "I have to get to
Boston tomorrow without anyone knowing."

"What for?"

"I . . . I can't say."

"You 'spect me to help you, but you can't say what
for? Forget it!"

Joshua looked straight at Hogan. "I'm going to George's Island."

"To see that John Meadows?"

"They'll be sending him back south any day. I want to see him before he goes."

"Forget it, Josh. Just forget it. I ain't havin' nothin' to do with no Reb!"

"He already knows about you, Hogan."

"What do you mean?"

"I told him about you in my letters."

Hogan's jaw dropped. "You did what?"

"I told him all about you."

"How could . . . what did you say?"

"You know, . . . how we do things together."

Hogan stared at Joshua. "What did he say?"

"He said he had a friend like you in Alabama."

The hardness in Hogan's face began to fade. "Your uncle know 'bout this?" he asked.

"No. He said visitors can't go to the island. But I know if I get there, he'll have to let me see him."

"Yeah, well, if the guards get you first, they're gonna think you're tryin' to smuggle somethin' in or tryin' to help someone escape. They'll shoot ya!"

Joshua released his grip on Hogan's shoulders. "I've been working on a plan to get myself out there."

"It's awful risky," Hogan said hesitantly. "Awful risky."

"Maybe."

Hogan took a deep breath. "I don't know, Josh."

"Think about it, Hogan. If you want to help me, meet me outside my house tomorrow morning at six o'clock."

Joshua turned and threaded his way through the crowd. As he left the square, he glanced back at Hogan standing in the glow of the bonfire. Hogan's eyes had not left him.

Chapter
Twenty-two

*H*alf past five. The time had finally come. Joshua snapped the cover of his pocket-watch closed and swung his legs over the side of his bed. The night had dragged on endlessly, and he had slept very little. Plans and contingency plans had streamed through his mind. There was so much to remember and so little room for mistakes.

Joshua lit his lamp, crept across the room to his closet, and opened the door carefully so that the hinges wouldn't creak. He pulled a good white shirt from a peg on the wall and then gathered his navy

blue trousers, his boots, and a pair of blue suspenders. He dressed slowly, taking pains not to awaken his mother in the next room.

When he finished, Joshua went to his desk and took out a sheet of paper. On it he scribbled a note to his mother explaining that he had gone to George's Island to see Uncle Robert and telling her not to worry. Then he took another piece of paper and folded it in quarters. On the outside he wrote, "For Major Robert Pennington—Private." He stuffed it into his pocket along with his watch and penknife and placed around his neck the binoculars Robert had given him. He turned down the lamp until the flame disappeared, and as quietly as he could, he descended the stairs to the front hall.

The sun had not yet begun to rise, and the quarter moon hung like a shiny saber in the early morning sky. At first Joshua could see nothing. Then, as his eyes grew accustomed to the darkness, he could make out the shapes of objects in the front hall and parlor. He groped his way to the large closet in the hallway. The interior was as black as a coal mine. He dragged his fingers across a row of sweaters and coats until he touched a heavy woolen overcoat. He pulled it out, threw it over his shoulders, and walked out onto the porch. By the faint light of the moon, he checked the time again. Almost six o'clock, and there was no sign of Hogan. His eyes searched the front yard for any

movement. But all was still and quiet save for the soft moan of the wind.

Joshua stepped down from the front porch. He waited. It was now after six. Hogan's angry, he decided. And he's not coming. Joshua would have to make the journey alone.

The morning air was brisk, but Joshua felt warm in his blue army coat as he walked to the square. His father had worn it in the early days of the war, and although it was a bit large, Joshua was surprised that it fit him so well. He moved rapidly, hoping to avoid any neighbor who would wonder what he was doing about so early in the day. His mind rehearsed the words he was sure he would have to repeat later that morning, the words that would bring him to Fort Warren. And John Meadows.

Except for a milk wagon and a farmer's wagon in front of Harrison's, the square was empty when Joshua arrived. He stood at the top of Main Street and gazed down at the darkened buildings that loomed like ghostly sentries guarding the town. The fears he thought he had left behind began to creep back.

"Don't turn tail now!" a voice whispered from the shadows.

Joshua nearly leaped out of his skin. "Hogan?" he whispered back.

A short figure emerged from a darkened alley. "I

knew you'd hafta come through here."

Joshua bobbed his head excitedly. "I'm glad you came."

"I was up anyway," Hogan said with a shrug. "Had to unload the papers from the early train." Hogan let out a low whistle as he drew near to Joshua. "Hey, you got on an officer's coat! You're a captain!"

Joshua panicked as he glanced at his shoulders. He had forgotten to remove the rank insignia from his father's coat. What a foolish mistake. He took off the jacket, and with a few quick cuts of his knife, the captain's bars fell from each shoulder. "There," he said, stuffing them into his pocket, "I'm a private now." He put the coat back on and looked at his friend. "I need to get to Boston on the train, but I don't want anyone to see me. And I don't want anyone asking me any questions."

Hogan wrinkled his brow. "I can probably get you in. But remember, if we get caught, I ain't no spy."

"Don't worry. We won't get caught," said Joshua, trying to reassure himself as well as his friend.

"Well c'mon!" Hogan said impatiently. "We don't got all day!"

The boys sprinted past the courthouse and through the square. When they reached the small rise that overlooked the railroad station, Hogan raised his hand and stopped. "Look!" he said, his eyes straining in the dim light of dawn. "That's the mail and passenger run

that goes to Boston. We gotta get on it, 'cause the later trains will be too crowded with the celebratin'."

Joshua stepped up next to his friend and studied the iron horse that stretched before him. The huge locomotive was spewing smoke and steam into the air. A tender car carrying water and fuel was coupled to it, followed by two passenger cars, a baggage car, and a mail car. Joshua's eyes traced the length of the train looking for activity, but except for a few silhouettes in the windows of the passenger cars, the only movement was in the cab of the locomotive. Just the engineer and fireman getting ready to go, he thought. He glanced down at his watch. It was almost half past six. "When does it leave?" he asked.

"A quarter of seven," Hogan replied.

"How we gonna get on?"

Hogan did a quick study of the area. "You see that tree down there? The big oak near the tracks? Hide behind it. When I give you the signal, run as fast as you can to the mail car. Now c'mon!"

As Hogan jogged toward the mail car, Joshua ran to the oak tree and planted himself squarely behind it. Trying to catch his breath, he peered around the huge trunk and watched Hogan climb onto the platform of the car and bang at its door. An old man, wearing thick spectacles, answered the knock.

"Hogan!" the old man exclaimed. "How are you doing?"

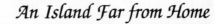
"So-so, Mr. Wright."

"Just so-so, huh?"

"Well," said Hogan sadly, "I was unloadin' the papers this morning on the Boston-Newport run, and I lost my watch. I was wonderin' if you seen it."

"Can't say as I have."

Hogan looked down. "It was my grandpa's old watch. My pa gave it to me on my last birthday. He's gonna be awful sore."

"Well, maybe you lost it alongside the tracks," said Mr. Wright, stealing a peek at his own watch. "Why don't we take a quick look."

"I 'preciate that, sir."

Hogan jumped from the platform to the ground. The old man followed after him on the stairs. "I'll look here," said Hogan, gesturing to the side of the train nearest the tree where Joshua was hiding.

"I'll take a look on the other side," said Mr. Wright.

The old man ambled around the car to the far side of the train. As soon as he was gone, Hogan waved his hands above his head. It was the signal Joshua had been waiting for. He made a mad dash toward Hogan. Hogan vaulted the steps to the platform and darted into the mail car. Joshua followed a half step behind.

Once inside, Hogan pointed to a cluster of large mail sacks leaning against the back of the compartment. They pried the sacks apart and jammed them-

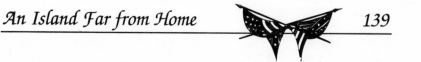

selves into the small space they had created. Joshua started to speak, but Hogan pressed his finger to his lips. "He's comin' back," he whispered.

Joshua held his breath. He could hear Mr. Wright's feet pounding up the platform steps. The old man was muttering, but Joshua could not make out the words. Just then, there was a sharp clanging noise as the door to the car closed shut. "Darn kid," Mr. Wright mumbled.

The old man puttered around the compartment for what seemed like hours but finally sat down. Suddenly a whistle screamed, and the train let out an enormous hissing sound and jerked forward. Despite his nervousness, Joshua found himself smiling. He looked at Hogan. There was a broad grin on his friend's face. They were on their way to Boston.

Chapter
Twenty-three

*T*he sharp squeal of brakes and the grinding of metal wheels against metal rails announced the boys' arrival in the city. Joshua peered above the mail sacks just as Mr. Wright disappeared through the door of the compartment. "He's gone," he whispered to Hogan.

The boys rose from their hiding place and kneaded the kinks from their cramped muscles. "Wait here," Hogan ordered. He climbed over the large, white bags in front of him and scrambled forward to the door of the car. "It's all clear," he said, poking his head outside the compartment.

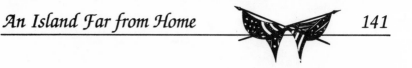

Joshua followed Hogan down the platform steps and into the railroad yard. Both boys blinked as the sun's bright rays reflected off the masses of metal and polished wood around them.

"Unbelievable," Hogan marveled.

Joshua could not have agreed more. The mail train had stopped on a track near two freight trains that stretched like colorful ribbons as far as the eye could see. Box cars, flat cars, stock cars were all poised to begin their trip south, carrying supplies and equipment to the Union armies in the field.

"Unbelievable," Hogan muttered again.

The boys weaved their way around the cars and past the station house. "I've got to get to the waterfront," Joshua said anxiously. "There's a boat there that goes out to the island."

"Which wharf is it at?" Hogan asked.

"I'm not sure."

"Probably Long Wharf . . . or Central," said Hogan, "that's where a lot of the boats dock. First we gotta find State Street, over by Fanueil Hall and the Custom House. That should bring us down to the water." Hogan pointed toward a large domed building in the distance. "There's the Custom House over there."

As the boys journeyed toward the waterfront, the name Fanueil Hall echoed in Joshua's mind. The last time he had been there was the day his father had marched off to war. His father's regiment had paraded through Boston Common and down the narrow cobblestone streets to the famous hall. The regimental band had marched first. Then came the officers, splendid in their blue uniforms, their swords dangling from their waists. Finally the volunteers had passed by, young men outfitted with the implements of war. Each shouldered a musket and wore a heavy belt that held a cartridge box, bayonet, and canteen. And strapped to every man's back was a heavy knapsack with a woolen blanket atop it.

Joshua remembered how much noise there had been. The cheering crowds. The rhythmic clumping of hundreds of marching feet on stone pavement. And the banging of canteen against bayonet. There had been speeches at Fanueil Hall, and the crowd had roared at every mention of defeating the Rebels. And when it was over, he had watched his father march past the Custom House to Long Wharf, where a steamship was waiting. He had never felt so proud. And so sad. He and his mother had waved good-bye, but he did not know if his father had noticed them among the mob of spectators. That morning was the last time Joshua ever saw him.

Hogan's voice cut the memory short. "You all right?" he asked.

"Yeah," said Joshua, "I guess so."

"Looked like you were dreamin'."

"No, not really."

"Josh," Hogan said, his voice filled with concern, "how d'you expect to get on that boat?"

"Gonna bluff 'em."

Hogan whistled. "If they catch you before you get to your uncle, you'll be in real bad trouble."

Joshua wiped the perspiration from his brow. "I can do it."

The boys plunged ahead through a forest of red brick buildings. The city was awakening from its slumber, and everywhere there were signs of life. A bleary-eyed businessman jiggled his keys in a door lock and stepped onto the sidewalk. A ragged black dog darted from an alley. A coal man shoveled heaps of black fuel down a cellar chute. A horse-drawn omnibus rumbled by. Joshua's eyes took in everything but absorbed nothing.

As the boys neared the Custom House, the air grew heavy with salt and the smell of the sea. Joshua adjusted his binoculars so they hung straight on his chest and walked with Hogan the remaining steps to the cold gray waters of Boston Harbor. The plan was becoming all too real now. But there could be no turning back.

"There's Long Wharf," said Hogan, pointing.

Joshua stepped up on a rock wall and looked out over the water. The wharf jutted like a stubby finger into the harbor. Sailing vessels and steamships were tied securely to it, and crews were busy loading and unloading their wares. So many ships, Joshua thought, but only one goes to George's Island.

As the boys contemplated their next move, a group of rugged-looking sailors sauntered by. "Wait here," Joshua ordered Hogan. "I'll be right back." He turned and ran toward the men. "Excuse me!" he shouted. "Hey!"

One of the sailors, a man with a ruddy, weather-beaten face, took a step forward. "You want us?" he growled.

"Ah . . . yes," Joshua sputtered as he drew near. "Yes, sir."

The other men began to chuckle. "Ya hear that, Jim?" said a short, solid-looking sailor to the ruddy-faced man. "He called ya *sir*. Ain't no one ever called ya *sir* before!"

Jim smiled. "What d'ya want, fella?" he asked.

Joshua pulled himself to his full height. "I'm looking for the ship that goes to George's Island," he said.

The men exploded in a gale of laughter. "Ship?!" said Jim. "That ain't no ship. It's a bucket!"

"No," another sailor joked, "it's more like a floatin' clam shell. It'd sink in a puddle o' spit."

Jim gave Joshua a once over. "You a soldier, boy?"

"Drummer boy."

"How old be ye?"

"Fourteen."

"H'mmm. I was 'bout your age when I sailed with

Farragut in the war against the Mexicans. Sailed on
the *Saratoga,* I did. Right up to the castle at Vera-
cruz." Jim studied Joshua for a moment longer and
then turned to his companions. "What d'ya say, lads,
should we give this young soldier a hand?"

"Sure," said the stocky sailor. "Why not help a fellow fightin' man?"

"Come on then," said Jim. "We'll show you where
the old scow is."

The men laughed and proceeded down the wharf.
Joshua gave Hogan a nervous glance but continued on
with the sailors. Although his hands were still shaking, he was relieved. He had passed his first test. The
men had believed he was a soldier.

The wharf vibrated with activity. Sailors scrambled
across the hard wooden decks of their ships, following
the orders yelled by their officers. Longshoremen
strained against ropes that lowered precious cargo from
the boats to the wharf. Passengers formed lines to buy
tickets to New York, Washington, and a dozen other
cities. In other circumstances, Joshua would have been
intoxicated by the sights and sounds of the harbor.
But now his mind was focused on one thing only—the
boat that went to George's Island.

"Well, there's your great ship," Jim said as they
reached the middle of the wharf. He swung his thumb
toward a tiny supply barge that was being loaded by
two soldiers. "Good luck, mate, gettin' to yer island,"

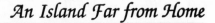

he added, slapping Joshua on the back.

Joshua thanked the sailors and turned to inspect the object of their ridicule. The barge was pitiful. It was no more than thirty feet long, and with each small wave, it pitched from side to side. But there was no other way to the island. Like it or not, he would have to go ahead. And leave Hogan behind.

He straightened his binoculars again and pulled from his pocket the piece of paper he had addressed to Uncle Robert. "Excuse me," he said, calling down to a young soldier who was loading provisions. "Is this the boat that goes to Fort Warren?"

The soldier looked up, a bored expression on his face. "One and the same," he said.

"I have a message . . ." Joshua started. "A message for Major Pennington."

The young soldier put down the crate he was holding and called to a slightly older man at the far end of the barge. "Corporal, the boy's got himself a message for the major."

The corporal moved lazily to where Joshua was standing and climbed onto the wharf. "So ya got a message, do ya?" he asked. "Who from?"

Joshua hesitated and then thought of a name he had seen in the newspapers. "Colonel Walters."

"Walters . . . Walters," said the corporal thoughtfully. "I've heard of him. And who are you?"

Joshua saw no reason to make up a name at this

point. "Joshua Loring."

"You're very young, Joshua."

"Yes, sir. I'm a drummer boy. I carry messages for Colonel Walters."

The corporal held out his hand. "Give me the message. I'll give it to the major."

"No . . . no, sir," Joshua faltered. "It's personal, and Colonel Walters ordered me to give it to him direct. See," he added, holding up the paper in front of the corporal. "It's private."

The corporal stared at the paper with a puzzled expression. Then he called to the young soldier who was loading the last of the crates. "Smithson, come here and tell me what this says."

The young soldier climbed out of the barge and looked at the paper in Joshua's hand. "It says, 'For Major Robert Pennington—Private.'"

The corporal nodded. "All right, sit there," he said, gesturing to a pile of food crates in the stern of the barge. "We'll take ya out."

Joshua dropped himself into the barge and made his way unsteadily to the rear of the swaying boat. Before he had even found a place to sit, the corporal untied the thick ropes that secured the vessel. The younger soldier pushed off from the wharf, and the boat slipped into the choppy waters of the inner harbor.

Joshua looked back toward the city. The thick stone columns of the Custom House dwarfed the waterfront.

He strained his eyes to see if he could locate Hogan's tiny figure amidst the clutter and activity on shore, but he could not. After a moment, he shifted his gaze to the rough waters that lay before him. As the boat lurched forward, he began to relax. He had made it. Now all he had to do was find Uncle Robert . . . and John Meadows.

Chapter
Twenty-four

eorge's Island first appeared as a small dot in the distance, a tiny outcrop of green and white that seemed as small as the boat in which Joshua sat. But as the barge moved closer to its destination, the island grew in monstrous proportions.

"Almost there!" the corporal yelled above the wind.

Joshua heard the corporal's voice but could not drag his eyes from the sights unfolding before him. Fort Warren sat like a huge, sculpted rock in the center of the island. Its thick granite walls rose over twenty feet. Every several yards loopholes had been cut in the

stone so that sharpshooters could fire down on at-
tackers. Atop the fortress the long muzzles of Rodman
cannons faced Boston Harbor.

"Ya see the guns?" the corporal yelled again to Joshua. "Can sink ships up to two miles away!"

Joshua had seen pictures of Rodman cannonballs in
the newspapers. They were almost half as big as a
man. He could easily imagine one of the huge missiles
blowing a Confederate warship from the sea.

The corporal maneuvered the barge alongside a
wide, wooden dock and secured it to a piling. No
sooner had they climbed out of the boat than they
were met by another soldier—a sturdy man whose back
was as straight as a New England pine. The corporal
and the young soldier sprang to attention. Joshua did
his best to imitate them.

"Sergeant," said the corporal, saluting, "this boy has
a message for Major Pennington."

The sergeant returned the corporal's salute and approached Joshua. Joshua could feel the sergeant's eyes
studying every inch of his face and uniform. "You have
a message for the Major?" the sergeant demanded.

The sergeant's voice made Joshua uneasy. "Yes. Yes,
sir," he managed to say.

"Who are you, boy?"

Joshua could not look the sergeant in the eye. He
stared lamely at his feet, much as he did when Mr.
Rawson caught him unprepared to recite his lessons.

"Joshua Loring, sir," he said. "I'm a drummer boy."

"What unit?"

"I . . . ah . . . I'm with Colonel Walters."

"I asked what unit!" the sergeant repeated impatiently.

The confidence that Joshua had felt an hour before melted like ice on a hot summer's day. "I'm with the ah . . . headquarters."

The sergeant continued his inspection. "Why are you wearing field glasses?"

Joshua felt another rush of panic. He had not stopped to think how out of place binoculars would look on a drummer boy. His mind searched for a logical explanation but found none.

"Answer me, boy!" the sergeant demanded in a voice as cold and hard as the granite blocks behind him.

"In case I . . . I need them."

The sergeant stood stiffly, his hands clasped behind his back. "And why is a drummer boy wearing an officer's coat? Looks like the rank insignia's been cut away. The threads are still there."

"Colonel Walters," Joshua started, "he . . . he let me have his old one."

The sergeant stared suspiciously at Joshua. He did not utter a word. The silence was unbearable. Joshua could think of nothing more to say and was too terrified to cry.

"Where's the message for the Major?" the sergeant said at last.

Joshua reached into his pocket and removed the paper addressed to Uncle Robert.

"Give it to me," the sergeant ordered, extending his hand.

"It's personal," Joshua protested meekly. "It's for Major Pennington himself. I'm supposed to bring it to him."

The sergeant snatched the note from Joshua's hand. "Major Pennington's gone for two weeks," he said as he began to unfold the paper. "He was ordered to Boston this morning."

Joshua's jaw began to quiver. It had never occurred to him that Uncle Robert might not be on the island.

When the sergeant saw that the sheet of paper was blank, he shook his head. Then he held it up for the corporal and the young soldier to see. "*This* is the important message the boy says he's delivering."

The corporal gasped.

"I don't know what's going on here, boy," the sergeant said gruffly, "but I'm going to have to lock you up."

"No! . . . No!" said Joshua frantically. "Don't lock me up. I came to see Major Pennington. He's my uncle. He wouldn't let me come here. So . . . so I had to sneak in."

The sergeant lifted the binoculars over Joshua's head

and then turned to the corporal. "Take him away," he ordered.

The corporal grabbed Joshua's arm and pulled him roughly in the direction of the fort. "Please, sir," Joshua pleaded. "Please don't lock me up."

"Ya made a fool o' me," the corporal said angrily. "I'll not have ya do it again." He dragged Joshua past the guardhouse and through the sally port into the fort. Confederate prisoners in gray uniforms were exercising on the parade ground under the watchful eyes of their guards. Joshua stopped short.

"Let's go!" the corporal barked, almost lifting Joshua off the ground.

"But what will happen to me?" Joshua implored.

"Who knows?" said the corporal. "Maybe they'll send you to Boston for a trial. Or maybe," he continued, "they'll shoot you right here as a spy."

Joshua's head began to spin, and he could feel his legs grow weak and start to give way. Suddenly all went black.

Chapter Twenty-five

oshua shook his head from side to side, but the voices did not go away. Voices that spoke words that were so familiar, yet sounded so strange—so different. He shook his head again, but the voices remained.

"He's comin' to," a soft voice drawled.

"He one o' us?" a deeper voice asked.

"Don't know," answered the first man, "could be, but he's dressed like a Yankee."

Joshua forced his eyes open. He blinked and tried to focus in the dim light on the blurry forms in front of him. "Where am I?" he asked groggily.

"Take it easy," said the deep voice, "just take it easy."

"But where am I?" Joshua repeated.

"You're in cell six at Fort Warren. Looks like you're a prisoner."

Joshua's body tensed, and his memory began to return. He could see the sergeant at the dock. And the corporal dragging him across the parade ground. And then . . . and then the blackness that filled his head as he tumbled toward the earth. He pushed himself up on his elbows and looked nervously about. He was lying in the center of a large chamber. Narrow shafts of sunlight cut through the bars on the cell door at the far end of the room. Bunks and bedding lined the wall of the cell, and clothing was scattered across the floor. As his eyes grew accustomed to the dim light, he was able to make out the features of the two men crouched on either side of him. The man with the deep voice was older and had a black beard that was streaked with gray. The other man, the one with the soft voice, had a thick brown moustache that drooped over his lips. Both wore the uniform of the Confederate soldier.

"Who are ya?" the moustached man demanded. "Them Yankees been known to plant spies in heah, and as best I can tell you're wearin' a damn Yankee uniform."

Joshua could feel the man's breath burn hot on his cheek. He did not know what to say. If only Uncle

Robert would come back, he thought, he would fix everything.

"Who are ya?" the Rebel growled again.

"Joshua . . . Joshua Loring," he stammered.

The older soldier arched his brow. "What did you say?"

Joshua eyed the men uneasily. "I said, Joshua Loring."

"Joshua Loring," the older man repeated. "Where have I heard that before?"

Joshua lifted himself into a seated position. At first, he was bewildered by the way the older soldier had recognized his name. Then he understood. "I know John Meadows," he said quickly.

The older soldier slapped his thigh. "That's it! That's it exactly!" He turned to his moustached companion. "You know John Meadows? The boy from Alabama?"

"I seen him around," said the moustached man.

"I used to share a cell with him," the older soldier continued. "He was writing to this boy here. Was right friendly with him, if I remember correct. John even got a couple of letters from this boy's schoolmates." He looked back at Joshua. "Ain't your pa Major Pennington?"

"He's my uncle," said Joshua.

The moustached man stood up. "You telling us you're the major's nephew?" he asked.

"Yes," said Joshua.

"Then why in tarnation are you here?"

Joshua climbed to his feet. Although his head had stopped spinning, he felt as if he had walked into a dream. Two hours earlier he had been with Hogan on the wharf. Now he was a prisoner telling his story to Rebel soldiers. "I wanted to see John before he left," Joshua started. "I tried to sneak in, because my uncle wouldn't let me come here. He's not even on the island now. I lied to the sergeant at the dock about being a messenger, but I got caught. He doesn't believe anything I say. And the corporal said they might shoot me."

"What do you mean, they might shoot you?" asked the older soldier.

"The corporal—" said Joshua, his voice breaking, "he said they'd shoot me as a spy."

The older soldier looked at the moustached man. "George, they wouldn't shoot a boy for trying to break *into* prison, would they?"

George shrugged. "I doubt it, but with Pennington gone, anything could happen."

The older man put his hand on Joshua's shoulder. "If we can find John, he might be able to help you. He delivers bread for the bakery, and he can move about the fort."

George scowled at his friend. "Lloyd, why are you trying to help this Yankee?"

"Come on, George," said Lloyd, "he's just a boy. And so is John."

George planted his fists on his hips. "Well, I'll go to my grave before I help a Yankee," he said. He thrust his face into Joshua's. "You know where Atlanta is, boy?"

"Yes," said Joshua.

"Probably know it from the newspapers, don't you?" he continued. "Why, I bet they rang the church bells up here when Atlanta burned. I bet it was a real cause for celebration, wasn't it?"

Joshua felt numb. The bells in Tilton Square *had* rung after Atlanta fell. And he had cheered with the others. He had not known anyone in Atlanta. The enemy had had no face.

George's eyes flashed with anger. "Atlanta was my home," he said. "That's where my family lived. That's what you Yankees destroyed. I got nothin' to go back to."

Lloyd stepped between Joshua and his other cellmate. "George, this boy had nothing to do with Atlanta. You know that. And there's been sufferin' on both sides. I was at Fredericksburg when we whipped the Federals. There were so many dead Yankees in the fields, you couldn't see the ground."

Joshua looked at the older man, the man who was trying so hard to help him. The Rebel had been at Fredericksburg! He had been one of the enemy who

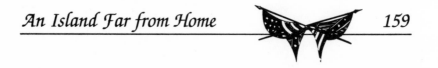

had fought his father. "My pa was killed there," he said.

Joshua's words took the soldiers by surprise. "Well . . .," said George, "that may be. But it sure don't give me no cause to help a Yankee." That said, he turned and stalked off to his bunk.

Lloyd remained with Joshua. "I can't blame George for feeling the way he does," he whispered as he watched his companion move away. "But this war sure ain't your fault, boy." He looked at Joshua. "I think it's important that you find John. I'll help you."

Joshua forced a weak smile.

"They'll be letting me out for morning exercise in a few minutes," Lloyd said as he walked to the cell door and peered through the small, barred window. "Then I do some work at the chapel." He pointed to the corner of the cell farthest from George's bunk. "Why don't you sit there and wait. I can't promise anything, but I'll do what I can."

Soon there was a jangling of keys outside the cell, and sunlight streamed in. A blue-coated guard thrust his head into the chamber. "If you men want to exercise, now's the time," he shouted.

Lloyd looked quickly at Joshua and then disappeared through the entryway. The chamber walls shuddered as the door slammed shut. Joshua crouched in the corner, lonely and afraid, waiting for John Meadows.

Chapter Twenty-six

*J*oshua's chest tightened when he heard the jailer's key scraping the hard metal lock. Lloyd had been gone for over an hour, and Joshua had not moved from his cramped position in the corner of the chamber. He glanced at George, now asleep on his bunk, then fixed his eyes on the door. He watched as it creaked open, and a shadowy figure slipped into the cell. He drew his knees close to his body.

"Joshua," the figure called softly.

"Over here," Joshua managed to say.

The figure moved swiftly to the corner, and as it

drew near, Joshua could see that it was a boy clad in Confederate gray, carrying a large basket.

The boy knelt next to Joshua. His face was filled with concern.

Joshua needed no introduction. The words rushed out. "John, I'm so glad you're here. I tried to sneak in to see you, but—"

"I know," said John, interrupting. "Lloyd Crawford told me what happened." John looked his friend in the eye. "Josh, I'm real glad to see you. I just wish it weren't like this."

The young Rebel plunged his hand into his basket and removed a bread roll. "Take this," he said nervously. "I'm supposed to be delivering bread. Don't want the guard to get suspicious."

Joshua took the roll and held it limply in his hand. "I'm afraid, John," he started. "My uncle's gone for two weeks, and the corporal said they might shoot me."

John shook his head. "I can't believe they'd do that." He paused, then added, "But it's something you just can't risk."

"What should I do?"

"Well," said John, "I haven't had much time, but I've been thinking up a plan."

Joshua clung to his friend's words.

"I got my orders," John continued. "They're sending me back home this afternoon."

"You're leaving today?!"

"Around three. They're letting some young prisoners and some sick ones go. There's going to be a boat at the dock to take us to a steamer in Boston."

The thought of being at the prison without Robert or John left Joshua stunned. "What will happen to me?" he asked.

"Listen," said John, trying to calm his friend, "there'll be about fifteen men leavin' with me today. We're supposed to muster on the parade ground. If you can get out of this cell for afternoon exercise, you might be able to mix in with us. I'll be there to help you."

Joshua looked down at his clothing. "But I'm wearing blue," he said. "It'll never work."

John pushed his hand into the basket of warm rolls. He groped for a moment and then pulled out an old gray jacket, a pair of gray trousers, and a cap. "These are kinda worn," he said, passing them to Joshua, "but they should fool the guards."

Joshua clutched the uniform with his free hand.

John reached again into the basket. This time he removed a battered haversack and placed it at Joshua's side. "Do you have a watch?" he asked.

Joshua patted his right front pocket. His watch was still there. "Yes," he said.

"Good. Put the uniform on. Afternoon exercise is at three o'clock, and a guard will come around. Tell

'im you want to go out. I'll be on the parade ground near the sally port. I'll be looking for you."

"But what happens when I get to Boston?" Joshua pressed. "I'll be wearing a southern uniform then."

"I know," said John. "The way I figure it, there'll be people and ships everywhere—a lot of confusion. Put your blue coat in your haversack. When we reach Boston, you can put it on. I bet you can slip away."

Joshua thought back to the activity he had seen that morning on Long Wharf. John just might be right.

As John stood up, the guard who had opened the cell door charged into the chamber. "Meadows, you're slower than a turtle in mud," he shouted. "You're supposed to be delivering bread, not making it!"

"I'm almost finished," John called back. He turned to Joshua. "I got to go."

Joshua struggled to his feet. "I'll do what you say, John."

John nodded, then he scooped a handful of rolls from his basket and moved quietly across the chamber, leaving bread at the foot of each bunk. As he left the cell, he called quickly to his friend, "See you at three o'clock."

Chapter
Twenty-seven

oshua pressed his face against the iron bars and peered through the window of his cell door. By craning his neck, he could see most of the parade ground. At the far side of the grounds, a group of Union soldiers was going through their drills, marching and turning and marching again, in response to their sergeant's commands.

Near the middle of the field, Confederate soldiers and their guards were engaged in a game that Joshua had never seen. A man was throwing a small ball toward another man, who held a wooden stick. When

the soldier with the stick hit the ball, he ran while the other men scrambled after it.

Joshua continued to scan the area. Directly in front of him, several dozen prisoners were stretching and bending their way through afternoon exercises. To their left, near the sally port, a small group of Rebels were forming a line.

Joshua removed his watch from his pocket. It was almost three o'clock. He smoothed the wrinkles in the old, gray uniform and waited. Soon he heard muffled footsteps outside his cell. A guard was approaching. He lifted his haversack from the floor and stood back from the door.

"Exercise time!" the guard called as he pushed the cell door open.

Joshua held his breath, hoping that his cellmate would not give away his secret.

"I ain't interested in no exercise," George croaked from his bunk. But that was all he said.

"Suit yourself, Reb," said the guard.

"I want to go out," said Joshua.

The guard eyed Joshua's haversack. "Why you carrying that?" he asked.

Joshua had expected the question. "I rest my head on it after exercises," he said quickly.

The guard grinned. "You're lazier than I am." He moved to one side and let Joshua pass.

Joshua tucked his haversack under his arm and

stepped out of his cell. He squinted in the bright light, then, as casually as his body would let him, he made his way toward the soldiers who were exercising. When he reached them, he drifted to the side of the group closest to the line of Confederates waiting to leave the fort. A single guard stood between him and the line. He dropped his haversack, lifted his arms in the air, and began to bend back and forth as the other men were doing. And with each twist of his body, he searched for John. A moment later, his eyes found him near the end of the line. The boys nodded in recognition.

A wave of panic rose suddenly within Joshua. How could John possibly help him? he wondered. How would he ever reach the line of Rebel soldiers? As long as the guard stood between them, the thirty feet separating him from John might just as well have been thirty miles.

Joshua looked again at his friend. This time John held a single finger in the air as if warning Joshua to wait. Then Joshua watched as John roughly shoved a thin prisoner standing in line in front of him.

The thin man spun around. "What did ya push me for?" he snapped.

"You've been crowding me," Joshua heard John say. Then John shoved the man again.

It was as if two angry dogs had been unleashed. The thin man lowered his head and rammed it into

John's stomach. John gasped and grabbed him around the neck, wrestling him to the ground. The Rebels broke from their line and gathered around, some cheering and others trying to pry the two men apart. The guard who had been standing between the boys rushed over to see what was happening.

Joshua saw his chance. He grabbed his haversack and sprinted over to join the throng.

The fight ended as quickly as it had begun. The guard fixed his bayonet to the barrel of his rifle and plunged it into the earth several inches from the thin man's head. "Break it up!" he yelled.

The men stopped thrashing but were still locked in a savage embrace.

"Get up!" the guard shouted.

John released his grip and rolled away. He picked himself off the ground and brushed the dirt from his uniform.

"You men get back in line," the guard ordered. "Any more fighting and you'll all be stayin' here."

As the Rebels began to reform the line, Joshua slipped in behind John and looked around quickly. The soldiers to his right had resumed their exercises. No one was watching him. No one had seen.

"John," Joshua whispered, "I'm right behind you."

John nodded but did not turn his head. Instead, he reached in his pocket and took out a tiny corked bottle. "I'm going to drop something," he said quietly.

"Pick it up." He opened his hand and let the bottle fall to the ground.

Joshua waited a moment, then, pretending to adjust his boot, he bent over and snatched the bottle from the grass. It contained a thick, reddish paste. Joshua cupped it in his hand and waited for John's next instruction.

"Rub it real good on your face," said John under his breath.

Joshua was baffled, but he did as he was told. He ducked his head, emptied the bottle in his hand, and rubbed the sticky substance on his face.

"It's something I made up with jelly and spices," John whispered. "It's supposed—"

Before John could finish his explanation, a tall guard approached the rear of the line and gave the order to march.

Joshua pushed the empty bottle into his pocket and fell in step behind John. He did not look to the left or the right, but stared only at the back of his friend's head. It was as if he feared that at any minute an enormous hand would grab him from behind and drag him back to his cell.

The prisoners marched through the sally port and past the guardhouse. As they emerged from the fort, Joshua could see a sailboat tied to the dock. In the distance a sleek schooner glided through the harbor, and a smaller sailboat bobbed toward the island.

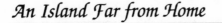

Joshua began to breathe more easily. John's incredible plan was working. Escape was only steps away. Suddenly, he saw something that sent a chill through his body. There, standing at the dock waiting for the prisoners, were the sergeant who had arrested him and the corporal who had locked him up.

Chapter
Twenty-eight

oshua could barely lift his feet, but his mind raced. Should he try to return to the fort? Should he make a run for the water? Should he go on toward the boat? A sharp pain in the center of his back answered the questions for him.

"Move it, Reb!" the tall guard ordered, prodding Joshua with his bayonet.

Joshua stumbled ahead.

The prisoners marched to a spot a short distance from the dock. The sergeant pulled a paper from his side pocket. "When I call your name," he com-

manded, "step forward." He glanced at the list. "Allen, Noah J.!"

A man near the center of the line left his place and trotted to the dock. The sergeant looked him over, crossed his name from the list, and motioned to him to go onboard.

"Buxton, Thomas R.!" the sergeant called.

Joshua watched as another man left the column and walked toward the sergeant. "John," he whispered, "those soldiers at the dock are the ones who locked me up this morning. They know me."

"Stay calm," said John. "Just keep looking down."

"John," Joshua started again, "what are we—"

The tall guard stepped forward. "Be quiet!" he ordered. "Just listen for your name!"

"Dalton, Horace K.!" the sergeant yelled.

And so it went. With each name called, the line grew shorter.

Joshua ran his tongue over his dry lips. The sergeant's list was alphabetized, and John's name would be called soon. With John gone, what would he do? Eventually, the names of all the men in line would be called. He would stand alone—a Yankee in a Rebel uniform. It was hopeless.

"Meadows, John S.!" the sergeant shouted.

"Don't say a word," John whispered to Joshua.

"Meadows, John S.!" the sergeant bellowed, this time looking up at the prisoners.

John took a step toward the sergeant and stopped. "I'm Meadows," he said. "And I'm supposed to be helpin' this sick man to the boat." He pointed to Joshua.

"What's your name?" the sergeant called to Joshua.

Joshua tugged his cap down.

"He can hardly talk," John answered quickly. "Got laryngitis. His name's Samuel Miller. He's with the Thirty-Second North Carolina."

The sergeant checked his list. "I don't see his name here." He stepped off the dock and came toward the boys.

"What's wrong with him?" the sergeant asked. "He looks all flushed."

"The doc says he had a fever," said John, "but that he's good enough to go now."

The sergeant stopped short. "If his fever's gone, then why is he so red?" he asked.

Joshua swallowed hard. John's plan was beginning to unravel, and there was nothing he could do.

The sergeant did not wait for John's reply. "Corporal," he said, returning to the dock, "go find Dr. Robinson and ask him if this Miller is supposed to be going home."

Before the corporal could take a step, a sailor who had been helping the Rebels to board the boat leaped onto the dock. "Hold on, Sarge," he said. "We have to get these prisoners to Boston before their ship

leaves! If you start hunting for people in the fort, they'll miss their boat, and we'll all be in trouble."

The sergeant tapped his pencil nervously against his list.

"It's getting late, Sarge," the sailor pleaded. Then he pointed to the harbor. "And we have to clear the dock for this boat that's coming in."

The sergeant turned his attention to the water. The small boat that Joshua had seen in the distance was now a hundred yards from the dock. The sergeant hesitated, then turned to John. "Put Miller in the boat," he said.

John rushed to Joshua's side. "Keep your head down," he whispered. He draped his arm over his friend's shoulders, and together the boys walked to the dock.

"Have him sit in the bow," said the sergeant, nodding toward the front of the boat.

John helped Joshua climb down into the swaying vessel. As the boys took their seats, some of the Rebels in the boat pulled back toward the stern. "I ain't catchin' no fever," Joshua heard one of the prisoners mutter.

The sergeant looked back at his list. "Peters, Edward L.," he called to the remaining soldiers.

"We made it," John whispered to Joshua.

Joshua could not respond. He was still gripped by fear, and the warm sun and the movement of the boat

made him feel lightheaded. Sweat covered his brow. He hugged his haversack to his stomach and tried not to be sick.

When the last Rebel was aboard the boat, the sergeant crossed the dock and stopped several yards from where the boys were sitting. "You all right?" he called down to Joshua.

Joshua buried his chin in his chest.

"At least you can nod, soldier," said the sergeant. "Look at me."

Joshua looked up for a split second.

A puzzled look came over the sergeant's face. "What's that?" he demanded, pointing to Joshua's cheek.

Joshua looked anxiously at John.

"What do you mean?" asked John.

The sergeant dropped to one knee and lowered himself into the boat. "I mean his face—it's covered with red streaks." He grabbed Joshua's neck with one hand and ran the other across his cheek. A sticky red film came off on his palm. Then, there was a flash of recognition. "You again!" he hissed.

The sergeant yanked Joshua to his feet and, in the same motion, sent him crashing onto the dock. He turned to John. "You're next," he growled.

John was not about to go without a fight. He drew back his arm, and with all the power he could summon, he buried his fist in the sergeant's stomach. The sergeant grimaced, but he did not bend. The punch seemed only to enrage him. He pinned John's arms behind his back and tossed him like a sack of grain onto the dock next to Joshua.

"Put them in a dungeon cell!" the sergeant shouted to the corporal.

Joshua and John exchanged horrified glances.

The corporal touched the barrel of his rifle to Joshua's nose. "Yes, Sergeant," he said.

Boom! A single gunshot exploded in the air and echoed over the harbor.

"Drop that rifle, Corporal!" a voice ordered from the far end of the dock.

The corporal turned defiantly toward the voice. Then he froze. "Yes, sir," he mumbled, letting his rifle fall with a thud.

Joshua sat up. The sailboat that had been making its way to the island had finally arrived. A Union officer was standing on the dock beside it. His revolver was pointed into the air, and a plume of smoke was rising from it. Joshua blinked his eyes to make sure they were not deceiving him. Then he jumped to his feet. "Uncle Robert!" he shouted.

Joshua broke away from the corporal and ran the length of the dock. "I'm sorry," he blurted out when he reached Robert, "all I wanted was to see John."

Robert put his arm around his nephew. "I know,

Josh," he said. "When I arrived in Boston, I saw your friend Hogan near the Custom House. He told me what you had done. I knew I had to get back."

Joshua nodded.

"I sent Hogan home to Tilton," Robert went on, "to tell your mother where you were, and so his folks would know he was all right."

The sergeant had the dazed look of a man who had fallen from his horse. "So this boy really is your nephew?" he said to Robert.

"He is," Uncle Robert replied.

The sergeant's face grew pale. "I'm sorry about all this, Major," he said. "Things have been real confusing around here. It's hard to tell who's a Reb and who's not."

"I'll take a report from you later," said Uncle Robert.

The sergeant raised his arm and pointed to John, who was now standing near the corporal. "Major, if that boy's really a prisoner, he'd better get on the boat. Time's runnin' short."

Robert beckoned to John. "Private Meadows, I believe you have a steamship to meet."

John's mouth split into a wide grin, and he scampered down the dock to join the others. When he reached Robert and Joshua, he pulled himself to attention and saluted smartly. "Thank you, Major Pennington," he said, "for everything."

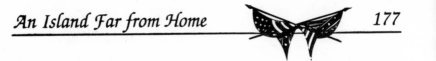

Uncle Robert brought his right hand crisply to his brow and returned the salute. "It's been my pleasure, Private." He smiled warmly. "Good luck, John."

John turned to Joshua. "Looks like we're both going to make it off this island after all."

For the first time that day, Joshua laughed. He extended his hand to his friend. "You want to keep writing?" he asked.

"You bet," said John as he shook Joshua's hand. Then his voice grew serious, "but first I have to find my folks. I'm not sure where they are now. I'll write you as soon as I can."

The boys retraced their steps to the boat. There, John balanced his foot on the edge of the dock and looked one last time at the fort. Then he took a deep breath, dropped to his knees, and eased into the vessel. As he lowered himself down, his jacket caught on a jagged sliver of wood jutting from a piling and a button was left dangling by a single thread.

"You're going to lose that," said Joshua, pointing to the small brass disk.

John looked down at his coat. "You got any use for it?"

"I can keep it for you."

John tugged the button from his jacket and passed it up to his friend.

Joshua held it in his palm. "It's got the letter *A* on it," he said. "What does that stand for?"

"Artillery," said John proudly. "The Confederate Artillery."

A soldier grunted and pushed the boat off from the dock. A sail of white canvas was raised and soon billowed with wind. Atop the mast the stars and stripes of the Union streamed majestically above the shimmering waters of the harbor. As the boat pulled away toward the toylike buildings that were Boston, John cupped his hands to his mouth and shouted, "I'll be seeing you, Joshua. You wait and see!"

Joshua tightened his fingers around John's button as if it were a precious gem. At that moment, there was no doubt in his mind that one day they would meet again.

Author's Note

Joshua's story is entirely fictitious, but it is set against the backdrop of actual events that took place during the last months of the Civil War. There is no town in Massachusetts named Tilton. Rather, it is patterned after several communities located on Boston's south shore. Today the cemeteries and war monuments of those towns stand as silent reminders of the sacrifices made by thousands of young men and women during one of our nation's most turbulent times.

During the Civil War, the huge guns at Fort Warren protected the city of Boston from the threat of Confederate attack. The fort also served as a training area for army recruits and as a prison for captured Confederate soldiers, sailors, and civilians. Conditions at the fort were very good, and the prisoners, who were as young as fifteen, were treated humanely. At various times during the war and shortly thereafter, over one thousand Rebels, including Alexander Stephens, vice president of the Confederacy, were imprisoned there.